APT   8

FIGHTING RAWHIDE

FIGHTING RAWHIDE

LEWIS B. PATTEN

30036010481784

SAGEBRUSH
Large Print Westerns

First published in Great Britain by Abelard Schuman
First published in the United States by Fawcett Crest Books

Published in Large Print 2009 by ISIS Publishing Ltd.,
7 Centremead, Osney Mead, Oxford OX2 0ES
United Kingdom
by arrangement with
Golden West Literary Agency

British Library Cataloguing in Publication Data
Patten, Lewis B.
  Fighting rawhide [text (large print)].
  1. Western stories.
  I. Title II. Patten, Lewis B. Sunblade.
  813.5'4–dc22

ISBN 978–0–7531–8254–3 (hb)

Printed and bound in Great Britain by
T. J. International Ltd., Padstow, Cornwall

To BETSY

in appreciation of the twenty good years

we have spent together

Part One: 1872

CHAPTER
ONE

I suppose that in my mind at least, the dry, sun-drenched fall of 1872 will always mark the beginning of the end for the monstrous institution of which I was a part, Sunblade Ranch. It has no end in the strictest sense, for it stands there still, sprawled out over three counties in northern New Mexico, covered with waving, tawny grass, and the dotted shapes of thousands of grazing Texas cattle upon whose hips are the circle and scimitar brand of the Sunblade family.

But the fall of 1872 began radical changes in our lives and in the relationships between us. Afterward, nothing was ever quite the same.

That fall, my mother went away. None of us realized it at the time, but she was never to return. And my father, John Sunblade, who had never been more than superficially tamed, began to change from the taciturn, often broody man he had always been, into a man of raw violence and sudden, terrible angers. No one, least of all I, can say what brought about the change. Perhaps the violence had always been in him, held lightly in check by my mother, a gentle, sunny woman who understood him and loved him well. Perhaps it grew out of events. But it came, and engulfed us all.

I was sixteen, that fall, going on seventeen. For the first time, my father put enough of his trust in me to send me riding across the endless, tawny grass to rep for Sunblade at Pegleg Johnson's roundup ten miles away.

Tom, my younger brother, rode with me, as I had ridden with Neil, my older brother, in previous years. And out of Tom's presence that day grew the hatreds that eventually threatened to destroy us all.

Tom was big for his age, spit and image of our father. His eyes were dark and arrogant, his mouth a wide, thin line in an angular face that had not been boyish for as long as I could remember. His eyes were reckless at times, but never for the sake of fun. It almost seemed as though, along with his mouth and eyes, he had inherited John Sunblade's angry, untamed spirit. That day, he seemed more restless than usual. He kept spurring his horse on ahead; then he'd wheel and return, the horse dancing and tossing his head against the pull of the bit. We had gone less than five miles before Tom said, "Dane, lend me your rifle. I bet I could get me an antelope up there ahead."

"What would we do with an antelope?"

"Bring it to roundup camp."

"And lose time doin' it? Huh-uh. Besides, they don't eat antelope on roundup. They eat beef."

"Well, a coyote then. Come on, Dane. Let me have it."

To this day, I don't know why I did. Perhaps things would have been different if I'd refused. But Tom had a way of going sullen angry when he was balked, and this

4

day was too good to be spoiled. I gave him the rifle and he spurred his horse and galloped wildly on ahead until he was out of sight.

Tom was young, probably fighting his youth, as all boys do. He longed for a chance to prove he was a man. Likely the high-powered rifle across his knees and the good horse beneath him gave him a feeling of power and strength.

Boys become men early on the Western plains. If you're not a man at sixteen, you'll never be one. But Tom was only fourteen. That was a little young, even on the plains. Too young to have much judgment.

I heard the rifle boom, much later, and from its sound, estimated that it was several miles away.

At first, I paid no mind. He'd said he was going to shoot something, and now he had. But as time went by and the distant roar of the rifle was not repeated, I began to wonder. Tom wasn't, never had been, a one-shot marksman. He hadn't the patience for painstaking target practice, as I had. I figured there should have been a shot to finish off whatever he had hit before.

Nor was it likely that he'd missed altogether. Because if he had, he'd have emptied the gun in his effort to make good the miss . . .

A strange sense of uneasiness began to crawl in my belly. Before I realized what I was doing, I had spurred my horse into a dead run and was pounding across the rolling grassland in the direction from which the shot had come. I didn't try to track; there was no reason for

5

it — then. I just rode as hard as I could, guiding myself on the sound of that single shot.

I had gone a couple of miles when I came over a little rise and dropped into a natural drainage in the bottom of which wound a narrow stream. There, in the bottom, were a couple of rickety wagons with ragged canvas tops.

A dozen people moved around them. Some were little kids. They seemed to be in the process of moving camp, which was odd, because it was now mid-afternoon. Usually travelers moved camp in the morning. I got the impression that they were hurrying. When they looked up and saw me, they stopped what they were doing and gathered into a little group to wait.

I rode down the slope, keeping my right hand close to the revolver I carried at my side. I nodded a greeting, and received a surly grunt from one of the men in return.

I said, "Any of you hear a shot?"

Their reactions to the question were mixed. The women — there were two of them — looked frightened. One of them shook her head. The other nodded. The man who had grunted said, "Yeah. Over there. Sounded about a mile away."

I looked around. I'd never seen sorrier-looking wagons than those two. The wood was weathered until it was ash gray. The canvas tops were in shreds. The gaunted horses must have been old and smooth-mouthed or they'd have looked better fed in this abundance of grass.

The people themselves didn't look any better. The men were unshaven, the women slatternly. The kids' straw-colored hair hadn't been combed for a week. Their faces were dirty, a couple of them smudged with tears. The women's eyes were red, as though they too had been crying.

I felt uneasy. I'd seen nesters before, but never such a sorry bunch as this. I grunted, "Thanks," and rode on out of their camp.

Something drew my eyes as I passed between the wagons. I glanced aside and caught a glimpse of a man's face peering at me through a rent in the canvas top of the second one in line.

Riding on, my spine crawled. I could almost feel the hostility of their glances behind me.

Father was always ranting about nesters — cursing them contemptuously. But somehow or other I'd never felt that way about them. They were people, like anyone else. I didn't see how their being farmers instead of cattlemen could automatically make them bad, while raising cattle made us good.

There was probably good reason for the hostility they had shown me. They were passing through cattle country, and had been for several hundred miles. It was easy to imagine the treatment they'd received at the hands of the cattlemen across whose land they had to pass. "*Move on — tonight. I catch you on my land tomorrow and you'll wish I hadn't. Don't let me catch you with any beef, either, or I'll hang your men from the nearest tree.*"

I was glad when I passed out of their sight in the rolling prairie. I halted my horse, turned and stared thoughtfully in the direction I had come. No wonder they were bitter and hostile. Nine tenths of the land they crossed belonged to the government which said it was open for settlement. Yet in practice, none of it was.

My thoughts returned to Tom. I told myself that my concern for him was unfounded. The kid was probably waiting somewhere up ahead. Or he'd gone on to Pegleg Johnson's round-up camp.

Downing my uneasiness, I rode on. My eyes kept scanning the surrounding prairie, but I saw nothing. About an hour before sundown, I rode into Pegleg's roundup camp.

It consisted of a single, canvas-topped wagon, a rope corral full of horses, and a loosely held herd of several hundred cattle. Pegleg Johnson himself had just ridden in.

He was a short-statured, grizzled man who was built like a bull. Usually clean-shaven, he had a stubble of graying whiskers today, and his round, ruddy, good-natured face was grimed with dust. His blue eyes were rather close-set, but they had a way of twinkling that made him look somehow benign, like a Santa Claus without a beard.

Pegleg's saddle had a special stirrup on the right side, a kind of built-in socket instead of a regular stirrup. Into this socket he'd shove the end of his peg leg, and with it he could ride as good as any man. Pegleg was a Mexican War veteran who had lost his leg, from below the knee, in one of the battles.

He grinned at me. "Reppin' for Sunblade this year instead of Neil, huh, Dane? You're growin' up."

I said, "Tom came with me. You seen him?"

Pegleg's face clouded. "No, and I don't much care if I never do."

I felt a return of the uneasiness that almost amounted to fear. I said worriedly, "He rode on ahead of me after he borrowed my rifle. I heard him shoot once, but I haven't seen him since he left. Somethin' must have happened."

Pegleg scowled. "He'll turn up."

"I'm going back to look for him. That bunch of nesters acted mighty damned funny."

His eyes grew sharp. "What do you mean, funny?"

"They were moving on. I asked them if they'd heard the shot. One of the women nodded and the other shook her head. But the man said they had."

I turned and started to ride away. I heard Pegleg mutter "Goddam that crazy kid!" Then he called, "Dane, wait a minute. I'll get a couple of men and come with you."

I waited, conscious of a stronger dread. Something must have happened to Tom. Otherwise he'd be here. Maybe right now he was lying back there on the prairie with a rifle bullet in him.

Pegleg rode out to the herd, spoke briefly to a couple of his men, and the three came riding toward me. The four of us rode out in the direction I had come.

Pegleg set the pace, which was a fast one. Once he called back over his shoulder. "We'll go to the nester camp, circle and try to pick up his trail. But we got to hurry. It'll be dark pretty soon." As we rode, the sun dropped toward the western horizon. The miles flowed behind us and the sun set, but it left the clouds in the west flaming with color for fifteen or twenty minutes afterwards.

At dusk we reached the place where the nesters had been camped but they were gone. There was only a litter of tin cans, bones, and a few broken dishes to mark their campsite.

Pegleg rode through the camp, studying the ground carefully. In one spot he halted, and stared hard at the ground. Then he said, "All right. Stay here. I'll circle and see if I can pick up any sign of him."

I rode over and looked at the spot Pegleg had examined so carefully. There were dark drops of blood on the ground, like when someone kills a chicken by lopping off its head, and holds it in one spot to let it bleed.

Scared, I circled the camp some more. Pegleg's two men rolled wheat-straw cigarettes, lighted them, and watched me impassively.

There was a little mound of loose dirt near the edge of the nesters' campsite. I dismounted and stirred the dirt aside with the toe of my boot.

It struck something yielding, and I felt chills crawl along my spine. My God, had they killed Tom? Had they . . .

Kneeling, I pushed dirt out of the hole with my hands. It was a wonderful relief when my hand uncovered a corner of a green hide.

I pulled it out of the hole and spread it on the ground, hair side up. The brand on it was Pegleg's, an odd brand that looked something like a wineglass.

The whole thing began to add up. Tom must have come on the nesters burying the hide. Maybe he'd tried to run and they shot him down. Right now, Tom Sunblade might be lying out there on the prairie somewhere . . .

Pegleg came riding into camp. He saw the hide and rode over to stare down at it. I said, "The thievin' bastards . . ."

He interrupted harshly, "I gave them that steer. Now come on. I've got a trail."

He rode away, the three of us following. I couldn't hardly see the ground, let alone trail, but Pegleg seemed to be onto something.

We must have ridden for about ten minutes when Pegleg suddenly stopped. He dismounted, and walked a circle ahead of his horse. Then he said, "Over here."

I slid off my horse and followed. It was almost dark, but there was a little light from the fading western sky. I saw Tom's body almost as soon as Pegleg did, and began to run toward it.

He cuffed me aside. "Wait. I want to see the ground."

"But Tom . . ."

"Tom can wait. I've got to know what happened. He ain't dead. I can hear him breathing."

He continued to walk slowly toward Tom, studying the ground. At last he said, "All right. Let's see how the kid is. Dane, gather up some dry grass."

I pulled great handfuls of grass and dumped them down near Tom's body. Pegleg struck a match. In the flare of the grass, I looked down on Tom.

His face was a bloody pulp, hardly recognizable as his own. His hair was matted with dried blood. But his chest rose and fell regularly.

Pegleg breathed, "Beat the livin' hell out of him!" He felt Tom's arms and legs gently. "No broken bones. But he's out cold."

I said furiously, "Wait 'till Pa . . ."

"The hell with that. We don't know what happened. Tom ain't shot, an' you said you heard a rifle. There was blood on the ground back there in the nesters' camp." He called, "Frank, bring your horse. You can ride double with J. W."

Frank led his horse over. They lifted Tom to the saddle and tied him down. Pegleg said, "Better to get him home quick, even if we have to do it this way. It'd take all night to get a wagon here."

He gave me the reins of the horse, with the caution, "Walk your horse all the way home. No trottin', understand?"

I nodded, mounted and set out for home. Behind me, I heard Pegleg say, "You two hightail it back to camp. I'm goin' to find those nesters. We'd better have a straight story on what happened before John Sunblade shows up with blood in his eye. If we don't, there's goin' to be more dead nesters layin' around than you ever saw before."

Then I was out of hearing. I rode the ink-black, empty land, filled with dread and a kind of fear I'd never known before.

12

I remember wondering whether Pegleg had told the truth about giving that steer to the nesters. A lot depended on whether he had or hadn't. If he had told the truth and if Tom had shot one of the nesters, there might be justification for what they had done to Tom. But if he wasn't . . .

My thoughts churned. At last I made my mind go blank and put my attention to getting home.

CHAPTER
TWO

The home ranch at Sunblade looked like a town. Built of adobe, there were upwards of twenty buildings altogether, dominated by the huge, sprawling, unplanned ranch house which had been added to, haphazardly, almost every year for as long as I could remember.

The original section was two stories high and fifty feet long. To this section had been added wings until now the whole thing formed a "U" which encircled a courtyard a hundred feet square.

Usually, even at night, there was activity somewhere among the scattered — sprawling buildings, Tonight, before I could dismount, there were half a dozen men around me, asking what had happened, and easing Tom from the saddle of Frank's horse. He was still unconscious.

Pete Hanley carried him into the house and laid him on one of the great monstrosities of oak and cowhide that served for sofas. The others clustered near the door, holding their hats in nervous hands and awaiting the word that would send them riding out into the night to avenge the wrong done to the youngest son of John Sunblade.

Mother came running into the room, to kneel beside Tom. She glanced quickly up at me, her eyes filled with fear and concern, yet somehow never losing her presence of mind. "Dane, bring a lamp close. Quickly."

I brought a lamp. She examined Tom quickly. Rising, she said, "Maria, some hot water and clean cloths. Rosalia, some pillows and blankets. Dane, go fetch your father. He's in his office."

I set the lamp down on a nearby table and hurried toward the rear of the house.

Father's office was in one of the wings, accessible only from the courtyard. I walked along the covered gallery until I reached it. The door was ajar. I pushed it open and entered.

Father sat behind his spur-scarred, littered desk. His reddish hair, now tinged with gray, was rumpled as it always was when he forced himself to do paperwork. It looked like the shaggy mane of a lion. His eyes lifted, blue and penetrating, and fixed themselves on me.

He boomed irritably, "What the hell . . . I thought you rode out for roundup."

"I did. Tom's been hurt."

"Hurt? What happened, horse throw him?"

"He got beat up."

Father came out of the chair. He topped me full two inches, and I was six feet tall. His shoulders were tremendous, pushing at the seams of his gray wool shirt until it seemed they must burst through. He said, "By God, talk straight. How the hell could Tom have got beat up riding over to Pegleg?"

"There were some nesters . . ."

I could see a vein begin to throb in his forehead. His face went mottled and his eyes were like bits of winter ice. "Nesters? Beat Tom? What the hell were you . . .?"

He was so overwhelming, so overpowering, that I couldn't help the anger that stirred in my heart. He never gave me a chance to finish a thing in my own way. He'd beat the words out of me like he'd beat the spirit out of a wild bronc, by the sheer force of his domineering will.

"I wasn't with him. He borrowed my rifle and rode ahead. I heard a shot. Just one. I rode in that direction, and found this nester camp. They said they hadn't seen Tom, but they'd heard the shot. I went on, and got to Pegleg's camp without finding Tom. Pegleg got a couple of men and we went back to look for him. We found him near the nester camp."

Father was already past me and headed out the door. But as he went out, I heard his angry, "Goddam Pegleg Johnson! The nester-lovin' son-of-a-bitch!"

I followed him. The crewmen still stood by the door, just as I had left them. Maria Sanchez and Rosalia, her daughter, huddled behind Mother, who was on her knees, sponging Tom's face gently with a damp cloth. She did not look up as Father came in, but I thought her back stiffened slightly.

He strode to her and peered down furiously at Tom. The vein in his forehead stood out, red and angry, pulsing with every beat of his great heart. At the door, the crewmen fidgeted and studied the toes of their boots. Pete Hanley watched Father with quiet, steady eyes. It came to me then that, except for Pete, they were as afraid of my father as I was.

His voice rumbled out. "Somebody'll pay for this! A fourteen-year-old boy! Good God!"

Mother turned her head to look up at him. "He'll come to soon. Wait and hear what he has to say. In the meantime, why don't you talk to Dane? Perhaps he knows something that will help."

Father turned his head and glared at me. Angry myself, perhaps feeling guilty because I hadn't been with Tom when it happened, I glared back.

He said intemperately, "Well?"

I stared straight at him. "The nesters were gone when I got back with Pegleg and his two men. Pegleg looked their camp over. He found some blood on the ground. I poked around and found a buried hide. It had Pegleg's brand on it.

"Then they were rustlin'. And Tom caught 'em at it."

I said, "Not so damn fast. Pegleg . . ."

An ominous quiet came over Father's face. "Don't curse when you talk to me!"

Everyone in the room stood frozen. There was a tension about them all. It was as though a wild beast was there in the room with them, and all waited fearfully to see which way the beast would turn.

I said defiantly, "Then listen until I finish. Pegleg said he gave 'em the steer."

Father uttered a single, obscene word. It summed up his contempt for Pegleg's word, for Pegleg himself, and for nesters in general. "Gave it to them hell!"

Mother stood up and faced him. Her face was pale. "John. Your language."

His glance swung to her furiously. I saw a clash of wills between them. My mother was a small woman, coming only to my father's shoulder. She met his eyes steadily in her quiet way. And slowly, almost reluctantly, the angry color left his face. He growled, "All right. We'll wait and see what the boy has to say."

He turned away, as though unable to continue meeting her eyes, and added defiantly, "But by God, if them thievin' nesters beat a son of mine, I'll hang every damn one of 'em!"

Mother didn't answer. Father strode to Pete Hanley, Sun-blade's foreman. "Pete, get some men ready to ride."

"All right, John." Pete was the only one I knew, except for Mother, who called my father John.

The crew turned and filed silently from the door. When they had gone, Pete followed them. Father began to pace up and down the room until at last Mother said, "Let us alone, John. I'll call you if there's any change."

He stared at her briefly, then swung and left the room. Outside in the courtyard, he resumed his pacing under the giant gnarled cottonwood that stood in its middle.

I sank wearily into a chair. A clash with Father always left me feeling drained and exhausted.

I thought of the nesters, of the fear that had been in their eyes, of their hopeless, beaten discouragement.

Already, I realized, my mind had worked at the problem until it had a believable solution.

I turned as Mother asked, "What do you think happened, Dane?"

"I don't know for sure. Probably Tom rode into their camp and saw the hide. He had my rifle. Maybe he got scared and shot one of them. That would explain those drops of blood on the ground."

"And then you think they beat him?"

I nodded.

"Do you think they stole the steer?"

I thought about that for a moment. Then I shook my head. "If they'd stolen the steer, they would have killed Tom and hidden his body. But if they hadn't, they'd be pretty damn — pretty darn mad about Tom shooting one of them. They're a sorry-looking bunch anyway. They looked like they were mighty near the end of their rope."

She nodded and turned her attention back to Tom. She was still a pretty woman, at thirty-nine, though sometimes there seemed to be something in her eyes that could only have been quiet desperation. I know she loved my father, though I've often wondered how she could. For he was a man I scarcely knew, and so could neither understand nor love. Of all those on Sunblade, Mother and Pete Hanley were the only ones I had ever seen stand up to him.

Often, when I was younger, I had wished that Pete Hanley, instead of John Sunblade, had been my father. Pete was actually more of a father to me than John Sunblade had ever been. It was Pete who put me on my first horse when I was four. It was Pete who bought me my first .22 and taught me to shoot. It was Pete to whom I took my questions and all of my troubles.

Pete came back into the room and closed the door quietly behind him. "Any change, Sally?" he asked.

She turned her head. "No, Pete. There's a bad swelling on his head. If he doesn't come to soon, perhaps you'd better send to town for the doctor."

"All right." He turned to go, but hesitated with his hand on the knob. A glance passed between them that puzzled me. He said, "Let me know if you want Doc." Then he went out the door and closed it behind him.

Tom stirred, and moaned softly. I got up quickly and crossed the room to my mother's side.

Tom opened his eyes. They looked frightened at first, almost terrified. Then they seemed to focus on Mother's face, and the fear left them.

She whispered, "Can you hear me, Tom?"

He nodded. She turned to me. "Call your father, Dane."

I went to the door that opened onto the gallery courtyard. I said, "He's conscious."

Father came striding toward me. He brushed me aside impatiently and pushed into the room. He went and stood over Tom, and for the first time tonight I saw his craggy, seamed face soften. "What happened, son?"

I watched Tom's face curiously. I wondered why Father was so blind to the things so plainly visible in my brother's face. It was almost as though I could look into Tom's mind, and see it questing, seeking, inventing a story that would best suit his purposes. Whatever came from Tom's lips, I knew suddenly, would not be the truth. Or if it was the truth, no one would know that it was.

Tom said weakly, "They beat me — them two dirty, stinking nesters beat me."

Mother said, with more sharpness than was usual for her, "Why did they beat you? Why, Tom?"

"Because they'd been rustlin', that's why. I caught 'em with a Sunblade hide in their camp."

A low growl came from my father's throat, but Mother persisted, "But why did they beat you?"

"Because I shot one of 'em, that's why. I threw down on 'em with Dane's rifle. I was goin' to bring 'em here. Then they rushed me an' I shot one of 'em in the arm." He looked up at Father triumphantly. "You goin' to go get 'em Pa?"

"Damn right I'm going to get them. I'll hang . . ."

Mother said angrily, "John, wait!"

"Wait, hell! I wait, and they'll be clear out of the country."

She looked to me beseechingly. "Dane says the hide had a Pegleg brand."

My hands were shaking. I said. "Tom's lying, Pa. There wasn't but one hide in that camp, and it was a Pegleg hide."

His face turned purple. He roared, "Why the hell would he lie about a thing like that?" I looked at his face. His eyes blazed at me. I had never seen him so furious with me.

Temptation was strong to back away, to let him go ahead, as he surely would anyway. And yet I couldn't help thinking of those ragged, beat-down nesters, who had probably done nothing worse than accept a beef from Pegleg Johnson.

Not that beating Tom up had been right, of course. He was only a boy. But when a boy packs a gun and uses it like a man, he ought to have to accept responsibility for what he does with it.

I said, "You don't want to face it, but Tom can't help lying any more than you can help getting mad. He's been a liar all his life. Right how he's lying because there's something here he doesn't want you to know."

He glared at me, switched his glance to Mother, then back to me. He was seeing, for the first time, I think, the similarity between us.

The realization of that likeness seemed to enrage him further. He came charging around the end of the sofa.

I wanted to run. I was only sixteen, still a boy in most ways. But I stood my ground stubbornly and met his eyes steadily just as Mother always did.

His arm swung, and the flat of his hand collided with the side of my face. I was flung aside, halfway across the room. My feet struck some obstruction, and I fell. My head brought up against the wall, stunning me.

I heard my mother's shocked voice. "John!" I struggled to my knees. I shook my head to clear it. The room fuzzed and blurred before my eyes.

Anger, terrible anger, surged through me. I fought my way to my feet. I would have attacked him, useless as it would have been, had not my mother's voice come to me through the fog of fury that clouded my mind. "Dane! Stop it this instant! Do you hear?"

I looked at her. Her face was white, shocked. Her eyes were filled with a nameless fear.

I nodded dumbly, then glanced again at my father.

There was no regret in his granite face, no softening in his eyes. He looked at me as though he hated me.

He turned and stamped wordlessly from the room, slamming the outside door viciously behind him. Looking across toward the stairway, I saw my brother Neil standing there, his face bloodless, his eyes scared. Behind him, a step above, stood Paul Lasher, whom Father had adopted years ago, after his parents were killed by Comanches.

Paul was smiling in the mocking way he had, as though it somehow pleased him to see such bitter strife between the members of the Sunblade family.

Mother left Tom's side, and came to me, but I moved away, avoiding her touch. I knew if I let her touch me I'd break down completely. I was damned if I was going to do that in front of Tom and Neil and Paul.

Her eyes were bright as she faced me. She said softly, "I can't explain him, Dane. But I can apologize for him, and I do."

"Somebody's got to stop him! Those people . . ."

"Yes, Dane. I know. Somebody's got to stop him before he kills them all."

CHAPTER
THREE

Neil and Paul Lasher came across the room from the stairway. Neil kept looking at the door nervously, as though fearing Father's return.

Neil was twenty-three. I know he feared my father, and I think he hated him too. He went and stood over Tom, looking down. An expression of shocked revulsion touched his face.

Neil took after neither Father nor Mother. His hair was the color of straw, and very fine. His face was thin, his cheeks hollow, his nose somewhat pointed and sharp.

His mouth was sensitive, almost as soft as that of a woman. Father had broken his spirit early and nowadays he took Father's orders meekly and without dissent. He avoided Father whenever he possibly could.

Lasher was a year younger than Neil, and feared Father not at all. He was smart enough not to tangle with him, though he seemed to relish the conflict between Father and me.

It is plain to me now that Father was disappointed in all of his sons. He had wanted sons in his own mold, tough and fearless and only half tamed, but had made such a thing impossible from the first. You don't make a boy into a tough, fearless man by breaking his spirit before he is old enough to resist.

Perhaps, in Neil, father saw the error of his ways. With Tom, he had reversed his tactics completely, coddling and pampering him until Tom knew he could get away with anything.

Neil said cynically, "So now he's going to hang a few unwashed nesters. Why all the fuss? If Pegleg hadn't given them the steer they'd have stolen it. And if they'd been on Sunblade at the time, it'd have been a Sunblade steer instead of one of Pegleg's."

I said, "The point is, they weren't on Sunblade and the steer wasn't one of ours."

Paul shrugged. "A fine distinction. That's the trouble with you, Dane. Why the old man's disappointed in you. It takes a man like him to hold Sunblade together — not one that debates right and wrong and is forever championing the underdog. To hell with the underdog. Give them a chance and they'll tear Sunblade apart like a pack of wolves."

I studied him. He was handsome, personable and likeable. He was smart. Everybody predicted that he'd go far, that when he graduated from law school it would be a short step for him to a seat on the Territorial Legislature.

But he was without convictions of his own, or principles. He was an opportunist, blowing the way the wind blew. I said sourly, "It takes a man like you, I suppose."

He grinned cheerfully. "I'll do until a better one comes along." He looked at Tom mockingly and said ironically, "Like him, for instance."

Tom got to his feet stiffly and swayed a moment, scowling at Paul. He seemed to know that Paul was baiting him, and he didn't know how to combat it. Tom was utterly without a sense of humor, and Paul often took advantage of it.

Still scowling, Tom turned helplessly and shuffled painfully toward the door. Mother moved as though to stop him, but I said, "Let him go. His head's too hard to hurt. Besides, he wants to see what he's started." I realized how much bitterness was in my voice but I didn't care.

Paul chuckled, "I want to see that too." He crossed the room and went quickly out the door. Neil glanced uncertainly at me and at Mother. Then he turned and hurried up the stairs. He could have been a whipped pup slinking away with his tail between his legs.

Mother looked at me helplessly. We were alone in the room now. Maria Sanchez and Rosalia had left. Mother walked to the window and stood looking out into the darkness.

It came to me with a sudden shock how frail she had become, like a slim willow shoot that stands the endless buffeting of flood and wind, yet always springs back as slim and straight as before. She had often bent before my father from necessity, but she had never broken.

Tonight, there was more discouragement in her than I had ever seen before. And something else — hopelessness perhaps.

She turned and looked at me beseechingly. She opened her mouth as though to speak, then closed it firmly.

26

I wanted desperately to help her, but I didn't know how. I wanted to take the burden from her, but I knew I could not.

I felt a tightness in my throat. She turned and crossed the room. When she faced me again there were tears in her eyes. "How are we going to stop him, Dane?"

I said, "I'll talk to him some more, but I don't think he'll listen."

I put on my hat and went out the door. It was as black in the yard as the inside of a closet, but down by the corral there were a couple of lanterns. The long, adobe bunkhouse was lighted up, and inside it I could see men moving around.

Father came striding toward me from the corral. I met him in the middle of the yard, turned and walked with him back toward the house. I said, "Why don't you talk to Pegleg before you make up your mind?"

He made a contemptuous snort, but did not reply. I insisted, "Then wait until morning. Even rustlers don't deserve to be yanked out of their beds in the dead of night."

Again he refused to answer. He stamped across the gallery and slammed into the house.

Furious, I lost my temper and shouted, "God damn it, listen to me! Do you think that if those people had really stolen a steer they'd have let Tom live? They wouldn't have dared."

I was just inside the door. He swung to face me the way I've seen wolves swing to face a tormenting dog. His face was twisted and strange; his eyes burned.

But I'd gone too far to stop. He was wrong, and somebody had to tell him so. I said, "What're you doing this for, anyway? To prove to yourself that Tom didn't lie to you? You know those beat-down nesters are no threat to Sunblade and you know they haven't stolen from you."

He lunged at me, and Mother stepped quickly in his way.

I don't suppose he meant to strike her, merely to brush her aside. But he was all raw violence, and his sweeping arm flung her helplessly out of his path. She staggered across the room and collapsed on the floor with a cry that was half surprise, half pain.

He halted momentarily and swung his shaggy head to look at her. There was a brief flash of doubt in his eyes. Then he turned purposefully back to me.

Mother was struggling to get up. There was a small trickle of blood at one corner of her mouth.

I knew it had come at last — the time when I must face my father and fight back or turn into another Neil.

I set my feet like anchors. Mother's voice was a small, lost cry, "Dane! Don't!"

My stance further infuriated Father. But it made him cautious too. He feinted with his right hand as though he'd grasp me by the shirt-front. Then, when I ducked, he flattened me with his left, balled into a fist that was hard as rock.

Stunned, I flew back as though kicked by a horse. I hit the floor on my back, groggy, but not quite out. He stood over me, trembling with a fury worse than any I had ever seen in him before. His voice was not his own,

"By God, boy, don't ever defy me! Don't ever do it again!"

The battle he fought with himself in the next few moments was plain for me to see. He paled, and trembled, while violence flared and rose in him like a prairie grassfire. Then, abruptly, he turned and flung himself out of the house, forgetting completely whatever it was that had brought him here.

I had lost, and Mother had lost, and both of us knew it as we rose from the floor. Mother's face was white and shaken. She dabbed at the blood with a fine linen handkerchief, and then looked dazedly at the red spot it had made.

She looked at me, a sorrow in her eyes that made me want to cry. She said almost inaudibly, "Dane, I'm sorry. Terribly sorry, my dear!"

I didn't know what to say. Without another word, she turned and crossed to the stairway. Her back was straight and proud and determined as she climbed to the top.

I was still unsteady from Father's blow, my mind in a daze. I staggered to the cowhide sofa on which Tom had lain and sat down heavily.

In the yard, I heard Father bellow, "Pete!"

I got up and crossed to the door. I opened it and saw him standing spread-legged in the middle of the yard.

Pete approached him from the corral, quiet and steady. Father said, "Send a man into Ashlock. Tell the sheriff I want a posse ready to go at daylight. Might just as well hang 'em legal."

Pete Hanley turned away and walked back to the corral. A moment later someone rode out in the direction of town at a hard gallop. The hoofbeats diminished like the rattle of a drum receding into distance.

I closed the door. It seemed in that moment as though my world were tumbling around my ears.

I heard a step on the stairs. My mother stood there dressed in a severe traveling suit of black. She looked like a frightened girl.

Her voice was low and throaty. "Dane, will you ask Pete Hanley to harness the buggy for me? Tell him I want Cigarette in the shafts."

Cigarette was her chestnut mare. I stared at her, but she didn't seem to notice. She turned and went back up the stairs. I thought her eyes looked too large and too bright, as though she were ill.

I went outside, and, avoiding my father, gave Mother's request to Pete. His face seemed to settle, and in the lantern-light near the corral, its lines seemed to deepen. But all he said was, "All right, Dane. Right away."

I returned to the house. Mother was standing before the big mirror against the wall pinning on her hat with a pearl-tipped hatpin. She said, without turning her head, "Dane, please get my valises from the head of the stairs."

I obeyed dumbly. When I had carried them onto the gallery outside the front door, she called me to her. "Dane, I'm a coward. I'm leaving. You can tell him it's for a visit with my sister Carrie and her husband in Denver."

I couldn't speak. She stepped to me and laid her soft cheek against my own. "Try to understand, son. It's not because he knocked me down. It's everything — every change that has taken place in him. He's not the man I married, and I'm afraid — God help me, I'm afraid. If I stay, I'll have to watch him kill someone."

I heard the sound of buggy tires on the ground outside. Mother heard it too, for she crossed the room, went out to the door and crossed the gallery to the buggy.

Pete Hanley helped her in. I picked up her valises and stowed them in the back. Down by the corral, I could hear my father shouting, oblivious of what was taking place up here.

Mother gave Pete her hand, and he held it for a long time, looking soberly into her face. She returned his grave regard, and in the faint light illuminating her from the doorway, I thought her face was slightly flushed. But her voice was calm and low as she said, "Goodbye, Pete. God bless you."

"And you, Sally," he replied hoarsely.

I climbed in on the other side and took up the reins. I thought it was sneaky to leave this way without telling Father, but I knew why Mother wanted it so. She couldn't stand another scene with him tonight. But as we drove out of the yard, I heard him bellow something unintelligible after us.

For a mile I expected momentarily for him to thunder up beside us, but he didn't appear. We drove in silence through the crisply warm night, across the endless miles of grass and brush, skirting sandstone escarpments and threading through an occasional thick grove of giant cottonwoods that bordered some near-dry stream.

It was past midnight when we drove into the wide main street of Ashlock. Normally the town would be sleepily settling down for the night. Dutch's Place, and the Ashlock Bar next door to the Ashlock Hotel would have been closing, and a couple of lonely drunks would be staggering home.

But tonight, such was not the case. Both Dutch's and the Ashlock Bar were going full blast. There were half a dozen or so men in the street before each of them.

I saw Dave Franks, segundo at Sunblade, the man Pete Hanley had sent in to the sheriff, in the middle of one group, the one in front of Dutch's. Then I drove on past and pulled up before the hotel.

I helped Mother to the walk, and she went into the hotel, her head high. I got back in and drove to the depot, where I asked if the one o'clock train was on time. Phil Morrisy, the station-master, told me it was.

He squinted at me from beneath the green eyeshade he wore. "Hear ye had some trouble out your way."

"Some. Tom got beat up by some nesters."

"Lord help 'em, they'll pay for that!"

"Likely. Stop the train when it comes through, Phil. Mother's going to Denver for a visit."

"Sudden, ain't it?" He peered at me curiously.

"She's been planning it for weeks," I lied.

I left him grumbling to himself, got back in the buggy and returned to the hotel.

She was sitting perched on the edge of one of the lumpy hotel sofas. She got up when I came in and crossed the white tile floor to me. "Dane, talk to Ace Wines. Perhaps he can stop your father."

I nodded, and started to sit down, but she said quickly, "Now, Dane. Please."

"All right." I got up and went outside. Across the street and down the block, there was a light in the sheriff's office. I didn't see what good it would do to talk to Ace. He was Father's man, bought and paid for. He'd do what Father said, no matter what anyone else happened to think of it.

There were a couple of men with him. I said, "Ace, can I talk to you alone?"

"Sure, Dane. Sure." He waved the others out.

He was a paunchy man, beginning to run to chins. His face was florid and laced with a network of purple veins, like threads in a dollar bill. His eyes were shrewd, slightly bulbous, and set close to his nose. He was a fine dresser, and always wore a flashy diamond stickpin in his tie.

Politician, more than sheriff, he controlled county politics by virtue of Father's support. He drank too much, but I must admit I never saw him drunk.

I said, "You've got to stop this some way, Ace. It's wrong. Tom lied about those folks having a Sunblade hide. It was a Pegleg hide. I ought to know — I dug it up. And Pegleg said he gave the steer to them."

Ace gave me a toothy smile. "Your pa tell you to see me?"

I shook my head.

His smile went patronizing. "Then you leave these things to us grownups, boy. Your pa knows what he's doin'."

"And you do too, I suppose."

Ace's eyes hardened. His smile faded. "What's that supposed to mean?"

"Take it any way you like." I turned around and stalked out of the office. I had wasted my time, as Mother had surely known I would. I'd go back and tell her, and she'd board the train, and what inevitably had to happen would happen. Two nester families would see their men killed. And all because an irresponsible fourteen-year-old kid wouldn't admit that he'd been wrong.

CHAPTER
FOUR

My mother must have known, when I walked into the lobby of the Ashlock Hotel, that it was no use, for she never mentioned again what she had asked me to do. She smiled, and I sat down beside her to wait.

She began to talk about coming to this country with Father, of the days when Neil and I had been younger and when Tom had been a baby. She talked with sad nostalgia about those happier, better days.

We heard the train whistle a mile out of town, and I got to my feet. She walked to the door, her back straight, her manner that of a woman going away for a short visit.

Down the darkened streets we drove toward the yellow clapboard station, smelling the dry corral of the livery barn, the pungency of sage out on the plain, the faint odor of the slaughter house at the edge of town. In our ears were the shouts of men in the saloons.

My face twisted. It was a lark for most of them, and they'd not go home at all tonight. They'd stay in the saloons drinking and carousing until dawn when it was time to go. They'd arrive at the nester's camp tired from lack of sleep, with the effects of the whisky they'd drunk rapidly wearing off. They'd be short tempered and mean, and not much concerned with right or wrong — only with getting it over with and getting home.

Mother bought her ticket as the train puffed into the station and screeched to a halt. The conductor descended and put a step before the coach door. Mother turned to look at me. I gazed down into her frightened face, for the first time in my life feeling stronger than she.

She said, "Dane, look after him," and then she smiled tearfully at the foolishness of the remonstration. She amended, "Look after yourself, son. And be as tolerant of your father as you can."

My throat felt tight. I felt tears coming to my eyes, and blinked. I put my arms around her and hugged her close.

She was weeping openly when she pulled away. The conductor said, "All aboard, ma'am."

I handed him her valises, and he slid them onto the platform. Mother was still crying, though almost without a sound.

The conductor helped her up the steps, then swung up behind her and gave the engineer the high sign along the length of the train.

Couplings drew tight like pistol shots. The engine snorted up ahead. The train began to move.

Mother waved forlornly, a white handkerchief in her hand. "Goodbye, Dane. Goodbye." And then she was swallowed by the night.

I watched the train until the white light of the observation platform was but a faint winking star in the darkness. And then I turned away.

I drove back down the street behind Cigarette, wondering where to go, wondering what to do. As young as I was, I realized what was happening to the men preparing for this nester hunt.

This was cattle country. Even those in the towns, who had no cattle and never would have, supported the theory of open range. To them, nesters were locusts, coming to devour, but offering nothing in return. It made them fair game.

I had another theory of my own. All men have their own frustrations. Periodically they have to be worked off. This business offered these men a chance to work off their frustrations against someone who couldn't retaliate.

I turned off Main and wandered aimlessly along the town's tree-shaded residential street. There was a light in Doc Trego's parlor as I drove past. Probably Doc was out on a late night call, and Anne was waiting up for him.

I pulled Cigarette to a halt, and for a moment stared at the house. There was movement on the vine-shaded porch, and a moment later I saw Anne standing on the steps, clad in something white.

She called, "Who is it?"

"Dane." I got out of the buggy, hooked the weight to Cigarette's bridle, and opened the gate.

She was in her nightgown, and had on a wrapper, which she now drew closer around her throat. "Is something the matter? Dad's gone out . . ."

"Nothing like that. Could I talk to you?"

She didn't reply, so I went through the gate and up the walk. I sat down on the second step, and Anne, after a moment's hesitation, sat on the step above me "What's the matter, Dane?"

I told her everything that had happened, including the fact that Mother had left for Denver. A faint, clean odor drifted to me from her, and I turned to look at her.

Her hair, unpinned for the night, was a cascade of midnight silk around her face. Her eyes were dark, shadowed, but there was no mistaking, even in this thin light, the expression of indignation on her lovely mouth.

"What are you going to do?" she asked.

I said, "There's only one thing I can do, and that would be both disloyal and foolish."

"What is it?" She had leaned toward me, and her face was only inches away. I had a powerful desire to close the remaining distance and kiss her, but I didn't. I said, "Ride out to Pegleg Johnson's place. I'm not sure he'd be willing to face Pa down over a bunch of nesters, but he might be willing to hide them. And he knows, if nobody else does, what really happened out there today."

She considered that and her face grew excited. "You've got to do it, Dane! You've got to! It's the only way."

"Pa would skin me."

"I doubt that. He'll blow and fume, but he'll probably be thankful in the end that you kept him from making a damn fool of himself."

It always startled me when Anne used profanity. She was a girl of sometimes startling contrasts; she could be warmly sympathetic and human, but she had a temper, as I had reason to know. And she had a quality of direct honesty usually associated by men only with other men.

She saw me staring at her and asked me what I was thinking.

My eyes didn't waver. "I was thinking I'd like to kiss you."

"Then why don't you? I'm thinking I'd like to have you kiss me."

I scooted up a step and put my arms around her. She was warmly responsive as I put my mouth to hers. But just as I began to warm up to it and lose my self-consciousness, she drew away. "That's enough, Dane Sunblade. Do you know it's one o'clock and I've got nothing on but my nightgown?"

I grinned. "Damn right I know it. You think I'm stupid?"

She said mockingly, "You better look out. Get me started and I'll . . ."

"You'll what?" I demanded.

"I'll run you ragged, that's what."

I reached for her again, but she evaded me, got to her feet and leaped away. "You've got something else more important to do right now."

I didn't reply, but I couldn't take my eyes from her face. I sensed the same excitement in her that I felt in myself.

She said, "Have you got a gun?"

I shook my head. I'd left my revolver and belt at home.

"I'll get you Dad's rifle. And you'll need a horse. You can take mine. Now get moving. Put Cigarette in our barn. Saddle up and come back here. I'll have the rifle ready, and something for you to eat."

I went back down the porch steps reluctantly. I drove the buggy around to the alley and up it until I came to Doc's ramshackle barn. I unharnessed and put Cigarette inside. I found Anne's mare, and an old hull that Doc sometimes used when he rode in rough country, and saddled. Then I led the mare through the yard to the front gate. I tied her to a tree.

Anne had Doc's rifle, a handful of cartridges, and a bundle of food wrapped in a clean piece of burlap. She also had a steaming cup of coffee, which I gulped down appreciatively. When I'd finished, I said, "Kiss me goodbye?"

She moved close. I put my arms around her and looked down into her face. Her lips were parted expectantly, but there was a devil of amused mockery in her eyes.

I kissed her, and suddenly felt the whole warm length of her pressing hard against me. Her arms went tight around my neck.

Blood pounded in my head. I felt as though I were drowning. I didn't even hear the clop-clop of hoofs on the street and so didn't realize they had suddenly stopped.

But I heard Doc Trego's gruff "So this is what happens when I'm out on a call."

I jumped away so quickly that Anne nearly fell. My face was hot with embarrassment. Doc chuckled softly. "Little rough on him, ain't you, girl?"

Her voice was filled with suppressed laughter. "I'd have been rougher if you hadn't come along."

I said sourly, getting mad, "To heck with you both!"

I untied the mare and swung to her back. Anne laughed openly. "Don't go away mad."

I grumbled something and rode away. Looking back at the corner, I saw Doc and Anne watching me, his arm around her waist. I supposed they were both grinning like a couple of chessy cats.

Then I began to grin myself. That Anne was some girl. One of these days . . .

But I hadn't time to think of that now. I had to get out to Pegleg's in time to rouse him and his crew, and do something about the nesters before sunup. That would take some doing.

I dug heels into the sides of Anne's trim bay mare and she reached out into her long lope. I held her to it while the miles and the hours passed behind.

Dawn was a line of thin gray over the eastern plain when I rode into Pegleg's ranch headquarters. It consisted of an angular, two-storey frame house sitting alone on a knoll, looking as out of place as a bronco Apache at a neighbourhood social. Behind the house at the foot of the knoll were the corrals, covering several acres in themselves, the barn and bunkhouses, chicken house, and an assortment of other buildings necessary to the operation of a large ranch.

A couple of roosters were crowing at the dawn, and as I rode in, half a dozen dogs came bounding out, barking at me furiously.

I circled around to the back, and a man washing at the horse trough looked up to stare at me curiously. I yelled, "Pegleg up?"

He gestured toward the house without answering.

I rode up the back side of the knoll and dismounted at the back door. I knocked, heard Pegleg's wife call, "Come in," and opened the door. It was a huge, warm kitchen, lighted at this hour by two lamps, one on the table and one on a shelf above the enormous range. Juanita Johnson, Pegleg's wife, turned from the stove toward the door as it opened, and smiled warmly when she saw who it was.

I felt embarrassed as I stepped into the room. There was something very personal in Juanita's eyes, and something else that could only have been speculating appraisal.

She was a striking woman, considerably younger than Pegleg. I guessed she was scarcely more than twenty-seven or eight, though I knew her daughter, Chiquita, was twelve. Her hair was gleaming blue-black, drawn severely away from her face, and done in a bun low on her neck.

She wore, as she nearly always did, a full, flowing skirt that reached almost to the floor, and a silk Mexican camisa that showed too much of her shoulders and upper breasts. I realized that my eyes were taking all this in and flushed with embarrassment. Juanita laughed easily.

"Sit down, Dane, and have breakfast with us. Pegleg and Chiquita will be here in a minute.

She brought me a cup of coffee, deliberately bending close to me so that one of her breasts touched my shoulder. I jerked away as thought I'd been burned.

I was relieved when I heard Pegleg's heavy tread on the stairs. A moment later he came in, followed by Chiquita. Behind Chiquita there was a stranger, his arm in a sling.

Chiquita may have been only twelve, but her glance was just as personal as that of her mother, and very near as knowing, too. I quickly avoided her eyes and looked from Pegleg to the stranger.

Pegleg asked, "How's Tom?"

"All right."

"You didn't ride this far to talk about Tom. What is it, Dane?"

"It's Pa. He's all stirred up. He's got Ace Wines all stirred up too. They're going to lynch those nesters for rustling."

There was a sound like a growl from the stranger. I glanced at him, and suddenly recognized him. His was the face I had seen peering at me from the tear in the canvas of one of the nester's wagons yesterday afternoon.

Pegleg glanced at him. "Take it easy, Miller. Nobody's goin' to lynch nobody. Not if I can help it."

I felt instant relief. I asked, "What're you going to do?"

Pegleg frowned. "I'm going to eat first. Hurry up, Juanita. Put it on." We ate quickly. Juanita and her daughter kept up their wordless teasing of me, and I kept getting more flustered all the time. At last, unable to stand it any longer, I got up. I grumbled, "Can't eat no more. I'll wait outside."

Juanita giggled. Pegleg glanced at her and back at me, and frowned.

I went outside. The whole sky was light now, beginning to turn pale gold in the east.

After a few moments, Pegleg and Miller came out. Pegleg stood at the edge of the knoll and bellowed toward the bunk-house, "Riley! I want everybody that ain't at the roundup camp mounted and ready to ride in ten minutes!"

I asked, "What're you going to do?"

He looked at me soberly, but with chilly eyes. "I'm going to let your old man know he don't run the whole damn country. I'm going to let him know he's got more than a sorry handful of nesters to fight if he wants to fight."

There was a bustle of activity down at the corral by now. We walked down the slope. I led Anne's mare behind me, and waited while Pegleg caught and saddled a horse for himself and one for the nester, Miller.

A few minutes later we were mounted and lined out toward the nester camp. Pegleg seemed calm and sure of himself, but the nester was nervous as a cat. His face was drawn with pain from the jolting motion of his horse.

Once, Pegleg said, "That wasn't very damn smart, Miller, beating the Sunblade kid. Not that he didn't have it coming, but it still wasn't smart."

44

Miller spoke between clenched teeth. "It'd never have happened if I hadn't been out cold from the shot he put in my arm. Those two kids of mine . . . well, they can't get used to being treated like some kind of damned animal. Neither can I."

"But a kid fourteen years old . . ."

The nester laughed harshly. "You ought to've heard the way that fourteen-year-old kid talked. He used words I'd never heard before. How much abuse do you think a man can stand?"

Pegleg said, "All right, Miller. It's done now."

But it wasn't done, and their faces betrayed their awareness of that fact. They knew there was more to come. Miller knew cowmen from unhappy experience, but Pegleg knew my father. He knew there was about one chance in a thousand he could stop John Sunblade without somebody getting killed.

CHAPTER
FIVE

We rode straight into the sun, varying our pace from a lope, to a trot, to a walk, and then back again to a lope. The grass whispered and waved in a light breeze. Dust rose from the hoofs of a dozen horses coming along behind us.

Pegleg, Miller and myself, and Pegleg's crew would make fifteen men. Add the two nesters in the nester camp, and you still had only seventeen. I knew my father would bring at least a dozen, and there would probably be twelve or fifteen with the sheriff. Pegleg would be hopelessly outnumbered. By riding to the roundup camp, Pegleg could have gathered a few more of the extra hands he had hired for roundup, but apparently he didn't think he'd need them. He was counting, I know now, on a determined stand. He figured neither the sheriff nor my father was willing to shoot it out over a handful of nesters.

As the sun rose higher in the sky, its warmth increased, but nothing, not even a hot sun beating down on me, could drive the chill from my body.

I dreaded facing my father when he knew what I had done. I felt like a traitor to him, yet some obscure defiance in me would not let me admit that I had done wrong. For I realized that if I had stood idly by while he hanged those innocent nesters, it would have been on my conscience as long as I lived.

The miles flowed behind us as we rode straight as an arrow across the rolling grassy plain toward the nester camp. They had moved less than five miles from the place we had found Tom the night before, and were now camped atop a low escarpment overlooking a wide, dry stream bed.

The day, with its winy clear air, its bright sun, the tawny land stretching away to the horizon as far as the eye could see, made the impending violence seem unreal and impossible. Incredible, I thought, that on a day like this men would fight and die in pain, and bleed their last on the dusty, thirsty ground.

We scrambled our horses up the steep slope, picked through the low rimrock and came out almost in the middle of the nester camp.

They were a scared, defiant bunch, but some of the fright went out of them when they saw Miller and when they recognized Pegleg. My presence puzzled them, for they knew who I was, brother to the boy they'd beaten so savagely the night before.

Pegleg looked toward town. "There they come."

At first, all you could see was dust, moving like a pillar slowly across the vast and open land. Then, as it drew closer, it was possible to make out dots that were hard-riding horsemen.

Pegleg breathed a curse, "Look like they've got thirty men!"

Miller ordered the women and kids into the two wagons. He had his two grown sons put their backs to the first wagon in line and waited. Pegleg slouched in his saddle and rolled a smoke. He lighted it and peered through the smoke at his men.

"Don't a damn one of you touch a gun unless I do. Understand?"

He looked at me. "Old John won't like your part in this. I suppose you realize that."

I nodded nervously.

He grinned. "If he boots you out, I can use a hand."

I said shakily, "Thanks."

We waited, then, in complete silence, broken only by the shuffling and shifting of the horses. The galloping horde of horsemen crossed the dry stream bed, thundered up the slope and climbed out through the rimrock in half a dozen places. They halted their plunging horses in surprise when they saw Pegleg and his crew.

Father's face, unshaven and covered with dust, was white with fury. He looked hard at me and afterward ignored me altogether. Staring arrogantly at Pegleg, he tried to beat the man down with his glance. Pegleg met his stare steadily and without flushing.

Father bawled, "What the hell are you doin' here?"

Pegleg grinned insolently. "This is my range. What the hell are *you* doin' here?"

"You know what I'm doin', you nester-lovin' son-of-a-bitch! This lowdown bunch killed a Sunblade steer, and then beat hell out of my boy because he happened to catch 'em at it."

"That what Tom told you?"

"That's the truth! Now, by God, get out of my way while I do what I came to do."

Pegleg looked at the sheriff. "You in on this, Ace?"

Ace wouldn't meet his eyes. "I'm here to see that justice is done," he said pompously.

Pegleg laughed contemptuously. "I don't suppose either of you is interested in what really happened, but I'm going to tell you anyway. Sure, these people had a steer. I gave it to them myself. Dane saw the hide, and any of you that's a mind to can still see it if you want to ride back to where they were camped when Tom found 'em."

He paused a moment, then looked directly at Father. "The trouble is, Tom lied about it. He walked into that camp yesterday, saw the hide and jumped to a lot of damfool conclusions. He threw down on 'em with his rifle but he was so shaky that he pulled the trigger. The bullet hit Miller here in the arm."

I watched the Sunblade crew, bunched behind Father. They were beginning to shift uneasily, and I saw belief for Pegleg's words in their reluctant faces. But I also knew that if this came to fighting, they'd fight as determinedly as if they believed themselves to be right.

All eyes were upon my father, who was beside himself with rage. I could see his great hands tremble. I could see in his narrowed eyes the effort he made for self-control. His hands, gripping the stock of his rifle, were dead white at the knuckles. His mouth twitched.

He looked around wildly, as though realizing he had thrust himself into an impossible situation. His eyes settled on me, hard and cold, as though I were a stranger.

He asked harshly, "What side of this are you on?"

I glanced at Pegleg, then at Ace Wines. I considered for the first time my own position and how untenable it would be if the guns came out. I couldn't shoot at my father, or at any of his crew.

Without replying, I touched my horse with my heels and rode over to my father. A little past him, I reined in and turned. It was the hardest decision I had ever made.

Oddly, I had the sudden feeling that some of the danger had gone out of the situation. A taunting word, a smile from one of Pegleg's crew, and my father would still carry it through to the bitter end. But he was ready to turn away if he was not goaded further.

His voice was venomous as he glared at Pegleg. "All right. Here's what I'm going to do. You see that bunch of Pegleg stuff down there?" He pointed into the distance to southward, toward a small bunch of cattle grazing. "I'm going to take ten head out of that bunch. And for every Sunblade steer your nester friends kill from here on out, I'll take ten more."

He looked at Pegleg with cruel defiance. "You going to try and stop me?"

Pegleg flushed. His eyes were suddenly filled with furious anger. His mouth was a tight line in his grim face.

For an instant, I thought he would force the fight. But he looked around at the faces of his men, at the nester Miller and his two sons. He weighed the lives of men against the injustice of Father's demand, against ten head of cattle. And when he turned back, the fight had left his face.

I glanced aside at my father. A faint, triumphant smile touched the corners of his mouth. Arrogance blazed from his eyes.

I saw the change in him now, the change Mother had seen last night. I felt the same premonition which she had felt, the premonition which had made her leave. He was sick — sick with power, corroded with arrogance. And I knew, suddenly and surely, that if he continued he would destroy himself.

He stared at Pegleg for a moment more. Then he whirled his horse to face his men. "All right. Cut ten steers out of that bunch. And drive 'em home!"

Pete Hanley whirled his horse and set his spurs. He thundered down the slope toward the distant cattle, the crew pounding along close behind him.

Father swung his great, shaggy head for just one instant. He looked at Pegleg and said, "From here on, stay out of my way." Then he, too, swung his horse and pounded after the others.

I followed. But as I started down through the rimrock, I glanced behind.

Ace Wines and his posse still sat their horses facing Pegleg and his crew. Ace said something to Pegleg, then turned and rode away. The posse followed sullenly and reluctantly.

Pegleg, looking strangely alone in spite of the presence of his crew, swung his head to stare after us. I had only a brief look at his face and the distance between us was close to a hundred feet. But I had the feeling that something was gone from his face, something vital which might never be replaced.

Another man might have survived Father's humiliation and defeat of him. Another man might have learned to hate, and come back, to retaliate and avenge himself.

Pegleg did not. Father had broken Pegleg Johnson that day. He had ruined him, destroyed the self-esteem so necessary to any man.

But a sense of relief touched me as I followed Father and the Sunblade crew out across the open plain. Disaster and killing had been averted, for the time being at least.

Part Two: 1873–1875

CHAPTER
SIX

With deceptive peacefulness, the warm days of fall passed and cooler air moved swiftly down from the tall Spanish Peaks in Colorado. Sunblade's herd of nearly a thousand triple-wintered steers trailed north to the railroad, and for the first time, I went with them.

Pete Hanley ramrodded the drive, while his segundo, Dave Franks, stayed behind to rod the ranch. All the way north, Pete laid increasing responsibility on me, until at the last, I was practically directing the drive under his appraising, watchful eye.

When we had sold the herd, he sent the rest of the crew back south, but he took me into Denver to bank the money and to see my mother once again.

I had never been to a town larger than Ashlock, and was amazed at the size of this mushrooming prairie metropolis. There were hundreds of buildings, many of them built of brick and rising several stories into the air. There were people scurrying about everywhere, afoot, horseback, in buggies and in well-loaded horse-drawn streetcars.

Mother was living, with her sister and her sister's husband, in a large mansion on the hill above town, one with a wrought-iron fence encircling the tremendous lawn, and with a carriage house and stable in the rear nearly as large as the house itself.

Her face lighted like a child's when she saw us, and tears glistened briefly in her eyes. She embraced both Pete and myself, and listened, entranced, while we bought her up to date on the goings-on at Sunblade and in nearby Ashlock.

We ate supper in the elegantly imposing dining room of the mansion, served by a liveried waiter, who looked at our sweat-stained clothes and uncut hair with monstrous disdain.

Leave-taking was hard, and I could tell it was equally hard for her. Thinner than she had been at home, her eyes were much too large for her face, and held a new and haunting sadness. She made no mention of her leaving, or of coming back, and while she did not mention Father's name to me, I was sure she inquired after his health from Pete.

Riding home, Pete was moody and silent. And I understood at last something I should have realized long before. Pete Hanley was in love with her.

Therefore, all through the winter, and into the following spring, he kept me with him, riding across the endless miles of snow-covered range, staying nights in lonely cow camp cabins. And he talked, teaching me all that he knew of cattle, all that he knew of Sunblade and its strengths and weaknesses.

More than once he said, "It's biggest weakness is its size, Dane. Remember that. The very size of it is an invitation to every greedy pup that comes along. A man's got to be hard to hold it together."

Hard, I was thinking. *Hard like my father*.

Pete nodded, guessing my thoughts. "John Sunblade built it and held it together. But the time's coming when he won't be able to go on doing it. They're waiting for that, Dane, all of them. They're like vultures waiting for him to die or loosen up the reins."

I was silent visualizing vultures tearing at a cow-carcass out on the vast, open miles of Sunblade range. Pete's voice went on, his eyes sharp on my face, "Your brother Neil couldn't hold nothin' together. Paul Lasher ain't interested in the practical runnin' end of it. An' Tom's just a kid. Which leaves only you to run things."

I began to understand why I had been taken along on the cattle drive last fall. Why Pete had taken such pains to teach me the intricacies of Sunblade's operation, from the branding and castration of a new-born calf, to the financing of the Sheriff's campaign for office.

Pete, wiry, bowlegged and solemn, said thoughtfully, "Your old man was fit to be tied over that nester deal last fall." He grinned at me wryly. "But you're the only one of his whelps that ever showed guts enough to stand up to him. It's made a difference. Maybe he'll try and shove Tom in behind you later, but for now you're the one he's got his bets on."

I must have looked puzzled. I couldn't imagine my father relinquishing any control of Sunblade, least of all to me.

Pete said, "You weren't at home when your old man got Sally's letter sayin' she wasn't comin' back. You

57

were still over at Pegleg on roundup. But I thought for sure old John was goin' to die. I even sent for Doc Trego."

"You mean he was sick?"

Pete Hanley grinned. Whenever he did, there were a thousand tiny wrinkles around his sharp blue eyes. "Sick? No, not sick, though he damn near made himself so. He was mad, boy, madder than I've ever seen him before. I thought that vein in his forehead was goin' to bust for sure."

His grin faded. "Reckon Doc Trego must've thought so too, for he tried to make your pa take to his bed. Might just as well have tried to make the sun stay down. Anyhow, he told John, before he left, that it was slow down and control his temper or have a stroke and die."

The thought appalled me. I couldn't imagine Sunblade without the blustering power of John Sunblade directing all its destinies.

With the spring, with the coming of new green grass to the frozen country, our range was dotted with crews of men, gathering and holding winter-gaunted bunches of shaggy Texas cattle while they roped and dragged the calves to their branding fires.

Every man carried an iron on his saddle, and every time a lone rider would come upon a slick-eared calf, he'd rope him and build a tiny fire to heat his iron.

I will never forget that spring, neither the heady taste of authority, so suddenly thrust upon me, nor the burgeoning of new life from one end of the gigantic ranch to the other.

58

Fawns hid themselves in the bushy draws. Coyote pups snarled and growled playfully in their hidden dens. Calves frolicked across the greening plain, waving their tails in the stiff wind like tiny, white-tipped banners.

But there is another reason why I shall never forget that spring, for it was in May that Mother died.

One of the crewmen came galloping out to where I was, nearly a dozen miles from the house. His face was expressionless, but the minute I saw him I knew something was wrong.

He handed me a telegram. It was from Mother's sister, Carrie, in Denver and read, *John Sunblade. Ashlock, New Mexico. Sally desperately ill. Come at once.*

Shock and fear ran through me as I read it. I asked, "Has he gone?"

The man frowned. "He ain't goin'. Said somethin' about her havin' made her bed . . ." His disapproval was plain on his ruddy, freckled face.

I asked, "Neil? Tom?"

"Neither one of 'em is goin'. They wanted to, but the old son of a . . ."

I said harshly, "That's enough of that kind of talk! Is anybody going?"

"Pete Hanley is. He sent me to bring you word."

I roped a fresh horse out of the rope-corralled remuda and rode out, hard, for home. I made it in less than two hours.

Pete had a fresh horse ready for me. I had hoped to ride out without a scene with Father, but when I saw him coming toward the corral from the house, I knew it was no use.

His rough-hewn face was like granite, his eyes like chips of ice. "Where the hell do you think you're going?"

"I'm going to Denver. Maybe you don't give a damn, but I do."

The vein running diagonally across his forehead stood out in sharp relief. His face flushed, as it always did when he was angry. He said, "No, by God, you won't!"

Nerves began to jump in my arms and legs. He'd floored me once with a single blow, and he could probably do it again. Except that this time he wasn't going to get the chance. I said, "Don't try to stop me." I picked up a short section of corral pole. "I'll flatten you if you do."

His eyes narrowed. Muscles in his face began to twitch. And that terrible fire in his eyes seared me until I wanted to run and never stop.

It seemed like hours that we faced each other, bristling like hungry dogs. My heart thumped against my chest like a blacksmith's sledge. So high was the tension in me that my head felt light. I didn't know whether I could strike him with the pole or not, but I made a show of being determined.

He wasn't afraid of me. I know that. Perhaps he saw that if we fought this out we would be enemies as long as we lived. Perhaps, too, the weakness was already coming upon him. Or perhaps Doc Trego's words had impressed him more than we thought.

But something went out of his face, suddenly, and I knew the danger was past.

It gave me no pleasure to have forced him to back down before me. So I softened it as best I could in my agitated state. I said, "She needs somebody. The one she really needs is you. Why don't you come along?"

"No!" The word was like a curse.

He stumbled to the corral fence and leaned against it. The flush had gone from his face. Now it was covered with beads of sweat. I said anxiously, "Are you all right?"

"God damn it!" he bellowed. "Of course I'm all right!"

Pete Hanley touched my arm. "Come on, Dane," he said softly. "We've got to go."

Father glared at him. I wondered if he suspected that Pete was in love with Mother, or if he'd care if he did know. I mounted my horse and followed Pete out of the yard. Looking back at the gate. I saw that he had recovered and was walking slowly, almost reluctantly, toward the house.

We rode hard, with little concern for our horses except to be careful they didn't play out before we reached the next of the ranches along our way which would provide us with fresh ones. We covered more than sixty miles a day, and on the fifth day rode into Denver and went directly to the mansion on the hill.

I was afraid she would be gone, but she wasn't. When we walked in, her eyes kept flickering from our begrimed faces to the empty doorway behind us, and I knew she was watching with almost childlike eagerness for my father to appear. When she realized he had not come, an expression of hurt came to her face, an expression that is indelibly carved on my memory. I believe that in that moment I really hated my father for the first time in my life.

She tried bravely to conceal her disappointment and smiled bravely at us, but the stricken quality that had come to her eyes remained.

Her face was pale and gaunt, her eyes enormous and bright with unshed tears. Pete stood at one side of the bed with one of her thin, transparent hands in both of his, and I stood at the other. She closed her eyes, and a tear rolled from one of them across her check.

My own throat was so tight I couldn't talk. She opened her eyes again, made a ghost of a smile, and said to Pete, "Look after my men, Pete. Look after them well."

"I promise, Sally." There were tears in Pete Hanley's eyes that he made no attempt to brush away.

Mother rolled her head weakly toward me. "The ranch is your father's life, Dane."

"I know."

"Help him, Dane. You're the only one of our sons who can."

Help him! Right then I wanted to hurt him as he had hurt her. She must have seen something of this in my face, for her own clouded. She groped for my hand, found it and squeezed it weakly. "We — John and I both — failed somewhere along the line. We failed you and Neil and Tom as well. But don't fail your father as

I did, Dane. Because he needs you now as he never needed anyone before."

I was silent, but the weak pressure of her hand was inexorable. "Promise me, Dane."

I remember thinking that I would like, someday, to have a woman love me as my mother loved my father. Then I nodded. My voice was choked and strange. "I promise."

She smiled faintly and the pressure of her hand relaxed. She closed her eyes.

Suddenly my heart was like ice in my chest. I looked up at Pete now, crying as unashamedly as a small boy. Pete's face was twisted, too.

I looked down at Mother again. She seemed like a girl, sleeping peacefully, a slight smile still on her waxen lips. But there was no movement of breathing in her chest.

Pete released her still hand and came around the bed to me. He laid a gentle hand on my shoulder. "Come on, son. She's gone."

Numb and dazed, I followed him from the room.

Her funeral was simple, but never have I seen so many people attend any funeral, before or since. The procession of carriages was a full four blocks long. Mother had made many friends in the short months she had been in Denver, and her gentle spirit had enslaved them all.

Afterwards, Pete and I rode back to Sunblade along the same route by which we had come, only this time we traveled leisurely and the trip took twice as long.

The summer passed, without much change in the regular routine of our lives, and winter came. The months rolled past, scarcely marked in their passing.

Paul Lasher finished law school that spring of 1874, and passed his bar examinations with flying colors. Afterward, he came to Ashlock, where he opened an office and hung out his simply worded sign, *Paul Lasher, Attorney at Law*.

Tom, as wild and unpredictable as ever, began to frequent the town of Ashlock, and though he was still too young to be allowed in the saloons, managed to turn up drunk several times a month.

Neil stayed on at the ranch, gradually taking over from Father much of the paperwork necessary to the running of it. Neil bought supplies from the wholesale houses in Denver. He kept a running tally of the cattle Sunblade owned. He paid accounts and negotiated loans from the Ashlock Bank, and brought order out of the chaos that had formerly ruled Father's office.

Father himself, restless and broody, rode his domain, a solitary figure drawing more and more into himself as the months and years passed. There were some who said he grieved for Mother. Others scoffed, saying that no heart beat in his monstrous chest, that you couldn't very well grieve without a heart.

Very often, nowadays, I wondered precisely what Mother had meant by "helping" him. Did she mean to take some of the work load from his shoulders? Had she meant she wanted me to get close to him and help him with some of the turmoil in his mind? I didn't know. What I did know was that I couldn't help him by getting close to him. He wouldn't permit it. Whenever he saw me he'd scowl faintly as though the sight of me offended him.

Except for my promise to Mother, I would have left, I know, and found a life for myself far away from Father and from Sunblade. But each time I was tempted to do so, I would remember her face and feel again the weak, inexorable pressure of her hand. I would recall my words, "*I promise*," and would stay on.

These years were the calm before the storm. The seeds of destruction were there in the restrained violence of my father's nature, in the tremendous prize that was Sunblade, in the hatred born for it among many of the country's inhabitants. All the seeds needed was time before they began to send up shoots and bud and flower.

CHAPTER
SEVEN

Among those who criticize my father yet in Trujillo County, there are some who blame him for all the terrible things that happened. But I know their accusations simply are not true.

Slyness, devious dealing, had never been one of my father's failings. He was as direct as the pitiless glare of the desert sun in summer, as uncomplicated as the northers that come howling out of Colorado in winter's cold and endless months.

But with my mother's death, a long hidden facet of Father's character began to show itself again. It was greed — the desire to enlarge what was already the biggest ranch in New Mexico. He began to crowd and threaten his smaller neighbors. He bought outright a couple of their places, places which he didn't even need.

Paul Lasher shared his greed. Indeed, Paul had a greed greater than Father's had ever been. But it was Paul who introduced deviousness into Sunblade's dealings with its neighbors, though I am forced to admit that Father sometimes acquiesced after the steal had become an accomplished fact.

Perhaps he felt a need to fill the void in his life that Mother's death had left. And, in his unimaginative way, thought he could fill the void with land.

For a long time I didn't realize what was going on. I was busy, for one thing, busier than I had ever been in my life. Father was gone much of the time, to neighboring towns or ranches, to Denver or Kansas City occasionally, leaving more and more of the actual operation of the ranch to me and to Pete Hanley, the only one of his employees he trusted unconditionally. Tom was an added worry to me, and a month never passed but what I was called upon to go into Ashlock or to neighboring San Pablo, to get him out of some jam.

But I read the Denver papers. It was *Paul Lasher, prominent young attorney, attends Tabor Grand Opera House with the Hon. Edgar Sinclair, member of the Territorial Legislature.* Or *Paul Lasher, New Mexico Attorney, advocates Statehood for Colorado.*

There were items concerning his attendance at parties, items concerning his rising prominence in political affairs.

Other items aroused puzzlement in me. Increasingly, Paul was seen in the company of Pegleg Johnson. He attended the races with Pegleg. There were sly references to the presence of both at some gambling establishment, or in the fabulous bagnios on Market Street.

Back home, in Ashlock and in neighboring San Pablo, Paul was often seen in the company of Juanita Johnson, Pegleg's wife, riding across the countryside, driving his shining new buggy with more speed than

67

good sense, while Juanita sat beside him, attired in clothes envied but not approved by the good women of the town.

I mentioned Paul's new friendship with the Johnsons to Pete one day and he frankly admitted it puzzled him as much as it did me. "Mebbe old John don't read the papers, Dane. With all the hard-feelin' between him an' Pegleg, don't look like he'd approve of Paul seein' so much of them."

I put the matter from my mind, for there were other things to occupy me. With the influx of more and more settlers, we began to lose cattle. So did all the other ranches in the country.

Invariably the ill-feeling between Sunblade and Pegleg led each to blame the other for its losses.

Our crews, meeting in town, bristled and growled like packs of stray dogs. Occasionally there would be a fight between contingents of our crews. Everything bad that happened to Pegleg was blamed on Sunblade. Everything that happened to Sunblade was blamed on Pegleg.

I know now that I should have seen and understood what was going on. I didn't, however, and even if I had, I doubt if I could have changed the course of events.

Besides, I was busy with my own and with Sunblade's affairs. Anne Trego was eighteen, and if I had thought her beautiful before, I was now more sure of it than ever.

Many a summer evening I bathed in the creek and rode into town, arriving so late that most of the town was in bed. I'd walk with Anne, or just sit with her on the porch steps for a couple of hours, then ride back in the small hours of the morning so that I'd reach home by daybreak. But each of those trips was worth the effort it took, and I never regretted a single one.

Anne was as unpredictable as any girl I ever knew, a strange combination of womanliness, masculine honesty and common sense. One minute she'd be as affectionate as a pup, the next drawing away, knowing well how she had stirred me, but knowing too the consequences of stirring me further.

The summer passed swiftly, and the fateful fall of 1875 began. The fall of 1872 had been the beginning of the change in our lives, but the fall of 1875 saw the change take shape.

Paul had moved to a newer, larger office on the third storey of the Ashlock Bank Building. Tom had reached the point where he was scarcely ever at home. Seventeen now, he thought himself a man, and stayed at Mrs. Roark's boarding house most of the time. He traveled with a wild town bunch that carried guns, and adopted an attitude of conscious toughness and devil-may-care irresponsibility.

Father gave him too much money, I knew. But when I mentioned it to him, he said gruffly, "Sowin' his wild oats is all. Every kid with spirit does it. Give him a year and he'll settle down."

Neil, out at Sunblade, had grown prematurely gray, not only of hair but of spirit as well. His hair thinned over his temples and he seldom got outdoors, preferring to lose himself in a world of dry figures and dusty ledgers.

October came, windy and sometimes cold, and one day late in the month, Pete Hanley, who had been over at Pegleg with a portion of the crew to pick up Sunblade's cut from their roundup, came pounding into the yard at Sunblade, without the crew, without the cattle, but with a frantic urgency that brought me out of the corral where I'd been saddling.

He thundered up to me, dragged his horse to a halt, and slid from the saddle.

I had never seen Pete Hanley so agitated. Usually he was calm when no one else was.

He looked at me grimly. "Hell to pay, Dane."

"Why? What's happened?"

He rolled a cigarette, his hands shaking. "It floored me. It floored old Pegleg too. Damn it, it just ain't possible!"

"What isn't? For God's sake, Pete . . ."

He grinned weakly. "It's Lasher. Paul. He's foreclosin' Pegleg's ranch."

I stared uncomprehendingly. "You're crazy!"

"No. I wish to God I was. Ace Wines came riding in over there at noon. He served the papers on Pegleg."

"But how could he? Paul hasn't any money to loan."

Pete shrugged. "He got it somewhere. Maybe from John. Maybe John . . ."

I shook my head. "No. Father doesn't operate that way." I remembered the stories I had read in the Denver papers, about Paul being seen with Pegleg, at the races, at the gambling places and on Market Street. I remembered the talk about Paul being seen driving

70

around the countryside with Juanita, Pegleg's wife. There was something here that smelled awfully bad.

I asked almost breathlessly, "What did Pegleg do?"

Pete looked at me soberly. "I never seen a man hit so hard by anything in my life. His face actually turned gray. He almost fell into a chair."

"Was Juanita there?"

"Huh-uh. Just Pegleg, and me, and a couple of his crew. He just sat there in the chair like a sack of grain and stared out at the prairie while Ace read through his paper. Ace finally told him he had thirty days to vacate." Pete snorted savagely. "Thirty days to vacate what he built, what he's lived with all his life!"

"How much is the debt, for God's sake?"

"Seventy-three thousand dollars! How in God's name did Pegleg ever get in that deep? I knew he was drinking. I knew he was hellin' around Denver with Paul. But seventy-three thousand . . ."

"There's something rotten somewhere." Suddenly I remembered the day three years before at the nester camp. Father had broken Pegleg that day, broken something vital about him. Before that, Pegleg had always stuck to business and had done no more drinking than any other man. It was after that day that he started helling around in Denver and drinking so much.

Suddenly I hated my father, hated Paul.

Pete was talking, and I forced my mind to concentrate on what he was saying. "I've never seen a man so beat. It was like Pegleg was dead, there in that chair. He looked twenty years older than he had a few minutes before. It was like watchin' a man turn old right before your eyes. And then, by God, it began to come back."

"What began to come back?"

"The life in him. His face turned from gray to red. He began to shake all over. He looked up at me and his eyes were plumb crazy. I don't think he even recognized me."

"Then what happened?"

"He bellered for Frank Jennings. Said for Frank to saddle him a horse. Frank did and brought it up to the house for him. Frank asked him if he wanted anyone to go with him, but Pegleg didn't even answer. He got on his horse and rode out like a crazy man for town."

I was moving almost before Pete had stopped talking. I ran back into the corral and finished saddling my horse. As I did, I told Pete, "Saddle up a fresh horse and come with me. Pegleg needs help — bad. If somebody doesn't give it to him, he's goin' to be dead."

Pete began to strip his saddle off his lathered horse. I sprinted for the house, calling back, "Saddle one for Pa, too."

Pa was in his office. I burst in without knocking. "Do you know anything about Paul foreclosing on Pegleg?"

His expression of pure amazement told me he did not. "Are you crazy?" he asked harshly.

"I'm not, but somebody is. Pegleg's headed for town with blood in his eyes. He'll either kill Paul or Paul will kill him, and I wouldn't lay a bet as to which way it'll go. Except if you think anything of Paul, you better get a move on."

72

I turned and ran from the house, with Father pounding ponderously along behind. A few moments later we were lined out at a hard run for town.

There was time to think now, and to feel amazement that such a thing could have happened. I was convinced that Father had had nothing to do with it. It was Paul.

But where had Paul gotten that much money? And how had he managed to get Pegleg to borrow it? I knew Pegleg had been spending heavily in Denver. I knew that rustlers had been hitting him and that he'd had to borrow on his place. But I'd no idea, nor had anyone else, that he'd borrowed from Paul, or that it had been this bad.

Fortunately, Sunblade was closer to Ashlock than Pegleg was. But I knew it wasn't close enough. Pete had ridden home from Pegleg, and now we had to ride to town. Combined, the two distances were greater than the distance from Pegleg to Ashlock, so it was likely that Pegleg would arrive before we did.

I hoped that Paul would have enough sense to stay out of Pegleg's way until somebody had cooled him down. Or that Ace Wines would throw Pegleg in jail.

By the time we reached town, our horses were blowing and lathered heavily on necks and shoulders. We pounded down Main and pulled up to a plunging halt in front of Dutch's Place. Pete swung down and crossed the walk at a run. He lunged inside.

He was back in an instant. "Not there. He must be at the Ashlock Bar."

I said, "One of us ought to see Ace. Pegleg won't listen to us."

Pete said, "Good idea. You do that, Dane."

Father looked from one to the other of us sullenly. "I don't know what the hell I'm doin' here. I don't give a damn what happens to that nester-lover."

Neither Pete nor I answered him. I whirled my horse while Pete was mounting, and thundered up the street to the sheriff's office.

It was locked, the shades drawn. I beat on the door for a few moments, but heard no sound inside. Discouraged, I turned away.

There was a shout down by the Ashlock. I swung my head to look, and saw Pegleg come backward out of the swinging doors as though thrown by a horse.

He lit on his butt in the street, and slid for several feet before he began to roll. He stopped, came to his feet, and his hand went for the gun at his side.

It wasn't there. It lay in the dust where he had landed. He made a dive for it, but Father, who was now on the walk, beat him to it and kicked it away.

Pegleg was beside himself with fury. His stocky frame shook with it, visible even to me halfway up the street. He screeched in a voice that did not sound like his own. "You filthy thievin' son-of-a-bitch! You're behind this goddam steal! But you'll get nothin' out of it, because I'll kill you and Paul Lasher and Ace Wines too before I'll give up my place!"

I swung to my horse, wheeled him around and galloped down the street. I put the horse directly between the two of them, but Pa snatched my quirt from the horn and laid it savagely across my horse's rump.

74

The animal, only half broke anyway, must have jumped ten feet. Then he bowed his neck and began to pitch.

I was busy as hell for the next couple of minutes, but I rode him out without letting him travel more than a hundred yards from the front door of the saloon. As soon as I could, I reined him back.

I was glad to swing down. The pitching had jarred me. But by now the fight between Pegleg and Father had gone too far to be stopped. The pair of them were rolling in the street dust before the Ashlock like a couple of boys scrapping in a schoolyard.

The sun beat down hotly upon them and dust rose in a cloud. Kicking, clawing, kneeing, they rolled toward the middle of the street, the two biggest men in the country, rolling around in the dust like a pair of drunken cowpunchers.

A horse, pulling a buggy down the street, saw them and reared in his shafts. Then he whirled and galloped away, with the driver, a woman, sawing frantically on the reins.

Father was larger than Pegleg, and more powerful. But Pegleg was fighting from a sense of outrage, which gave him a strength not matched by that of men when in their saner moments.

They clawed and heaved in the dirt for several moments, then they rose to their feet and began to slug it out. All the time Pegleg kept panting through bloody lips, "You dirty, thievin', sneaky son-of-a-bitch! By God, I'll show you!"

At first, Father had fought Pegleg grimly but calmly, the way he fought weather, adversity, a wild horse or anything else. But Pegleg's taunting gradually got to him. I saw his face begin to flush. I saw the narrowing of his eyes. I saw the vein in his forehead swell and begin to pulse wildly. But I knew there was no more chance of stopping this than there was of halting a tornado wind.

People continued to gather from all parts of the town as news of the fight spread, until at the last there were nearly a hundred people silently watching there in the street.

Pegleg's mouth was smashed and swelled until his words came thickly from it. Father had a lump nearly as big as an egg on his cheekbone, and a gash torn in his cheek. He was bleeding from the nose.

I heard Doc Trego's voice in the rear of the crowd, irascible and impatient, "Let me through, damn it, before he's dead."

There may have been doubt in the minds of the onlookers as to which of the two he meant. There was none in mine. Father had been warned against the uncontrolled run of his temper. Pete Hanley had told me he'd nearly had a stroke at the time he received Mother's letter saying she intended never to return.

So I watched him with a kind of hypnotized fascination. And then it happened.

He stiffened. His eyes rolled wildly, showing their whites. His mouth twitched, and twisted out of shape as though no longer under his control.

He drooled from the mouth, and made choking, incoherent sounds like some kind of wounded animal. Then, stiff as a tall pine, he tottered and fell with a sodden thud into the dusty street.

Pegleg looked down at him in pure amazement, still not understanding the nature of the thing that had felled him. Doc came pushing angrily through the crowd and knelt. He pushed back one of father's eyelids and peered closely. Then he turned irritably. "Don't stand there gawking, you blasted fools! Carry him to my house! Quick!"

I ran over and seized my father under the armpits. Pete grabbed his feet. A couple of others locked their arms under his thick middle.

He was dead weight, and ponderous, but we almost ran down Main and off to the side street where Doc Trego lived. We stumbled up the steps and carried him in. Doc, scurrying ahead of us nervously, directed us to one of the bedrooms where we laid my father's limp, dusty, unconscious form on the bed.

Doc was rolling up his sleeves. He said shortly, "Now get the hell out of here and let me work."

We filed silently out the door. In the street before Doc's house, the crowd, which had followed us, talked in subdued tones among themselves. It was almost as though a king had been stricken, a king hated by most, liked by a few, but respected by all for his strength.

Pete said, "Dane, I need a drink."

I nodded silently. Both of us had forgotten Pegleg in the excitement. Now we hurried toward the saloon with great, long, running strides.

CHAPTER
EIGHT

It was now late afternoon. The sun lay more than halfway down the western sky, magnified by dust in the air, partly obscured by a haze peculiar to autumn on the New Mexico grasslands.

Slowly the crowd began to disperse behind us. I asked breathlessly, "Pete, how does a stroke affect a man? Does he die, or does he recover?"

Pete shrugged. "Depends on the man, and how bad the stroke is. Sometimes a man recovers completely. Sometimes he dies. But he could live, crippled, for a long, long time."

I shuddered inwardly. I hoped Father would either live or die, cleanly, that he'd never have to live as a cripple.

Pegleg stood dazedly at the bar of the Ashlock, a drink before him. He looked at us blankly as we came in. I stepped over beside him. He looked at me wonderingly.

"I never even hit him. But he fell like he was knocked out cold. What happened?"

I said, "He had a stroke, Pegleg."

Apparently, he had picked his gun up from the street, for it was now in its holster. He pulled it out and laid it on the bar. He fished a red bandanna from his pocket and began to wipe it off. When he had finished, he inspected the loads and peered into the muzzle.

He looked at me dazedly, and muttered thickly through his battered lips, "They're takin' my ranch. They're takin' Pegleg!"

I didn't speak. There was nothing I could say.

His eyes slowly lost their dazed quality and began to show anger again. He turned away, looked at the gun before him and muttered, "But they're not goin' to get away with it. Not, by God, while I can hold a gun."

He shoved the gun firmly into its holster. He gulped the drink before him, poured another and gulped that. He turned, then, and headed for the door.

I didn't hesitate. I followed him, but I didn't try to catch up.

He crossed the street to the Ashlock Bank Building, entered the foyer and began to climb the stairs. I stayed about ten steps behind him but he didn't even look around.

I wondered where Ace Wines was. Trust the sheriff to be absent when he was needed. Probably Ace knew the foreclosure notice would blow things sky high between Pegleg and Sunblade. Probably he'd deliberately found something to do, miles away from Ashlock.

By the time we reached the third floor, Pegleg was puffing audibly, but I could tell he was getting angrier by the minute. His back was eloquent of rising fury, as was his quickening step.

He burst into Paul's office so ferociously that the door slammed back hard against the wall. He lunged inside, his hand going already for the gun at his side.

I leaped in behind him. Regardless of how I felt about this, I wasn't going to let him shoot Paul any more than I was going to let Paul shoot him.

I seized him from behind, and he swung his shaggy head, surprise in his eyes which said, "You too?" Then he was fighting like an infuriated bear to throw me off and clear his gun.

I caught a glimpse of Paul beside his ornately carved roll-top desk, startled, frightened. Then I was whirled around, and flung bodily over Pegleg's head as he grasped my neck and bent forward.

I struck an oak table leg, breaking it. The table, with its load of lawbooks and papers, collapsed on top of me.

I heard a shot, and struggling, managed to turn my head. Paul was grappling with Pegleg. He held Pegleg's gun hand in both of his own. As I watched, they fell to the floor, out of my sight now because of the overturned table.

I fought to clear myself but I was half buried under dozens of books and it took an instant before I could. Just as I came to my knees, I heard a second shot.

Frantically now, I lunged to my feet, and swung around.

Pegleg lay on the floor, limp and lifeless. Paul, his face white, his eyes terrified, was rising, the gun in both his hands. A wisp of smoke trailed upward from its muzzle.

I knelt beside Pegleg. There was a spreading stain on the front of his shirt. I seized his thick, hairy wrist and put my fingers on his pulse. There was none.

Paul's voice was a screech. "You saw it, Dane! He tried to kill me! But he shot himself instead."

I asked, "Then how did you get the gun in your hands?"

"I picked it up! That's all. He dropped it when he shot himself. I didn't know he was dead, so I picked it up!"

He was almost beside himself. Gone was his superior self-possession, his mocking arrogance.

I felt sick to my stomach. It wouldn't matter what I said. It wouldn't even matter if it were proved that he wrenched Pegleg's gun from his hands and shot him with it deliberately. Because Pegleg had pulled the gun, and Pegleg had fired it once. Whatever Paul had done could be said to have been done lawfully in defense of his life.

Nevertheless, one unalterable fact remained. Paul had murdered Pegleg, as surely as though he'd shot him without warning in the back. Paul had made it impossible for Pegleg to do anything but come here and fight for the ranch he had lost.

I doubted if Pegleg's debts to Paul were legitimate. But I couldn't prove they weren't. There wasn't a single, solitary thing I could do, because Paul held all the cards.

I looked at him, despising him, hating him for his greed, his unscrupulousness. Gone now was his fright, the panic that had gripped him at first. Now, he was smiling faintly, as though satisfied with a job well done.

And it came to me suddenly that Paul, with whom I had grown up and whom I had thought I knew, was more dangerous than either my father or Pegleg had ever been.

Because his only code was opportunism, and he had no moral scruples at all. First, he had taken Pegleg's wife, if the talk I had heard was true. Then he had taken Pegleg's ranch, under the guise of friendship. Now he had taken Pegleg's life.

I felt like gagging. A nagging coldness had begun to creep through me. I thought I knew where Paul Lasher would look for new worlds to conquer. He would look toward Sunblade.

CHAPTER
NINE

Now that the trouble was over, Ace Wines came puffing up the stairs and burst into the room. He knelt briefly beside Pegleg on the floor, then glanced at Paul, still holding the gun. His tone was respectful. "What happened here, Mr. Lasher?"

I looked at Paul, at Ace, and then at Pegleg on the floor. I felt disgusted and angry, and somehow unclean. I stamped furiously out of the office and down the stairs, knowing before I heard it how Ace's interrogation would go.

There was a small crowd at the street entrance of the bank building, held back by one of Ace's deputies. They all began to ask questions of me at once, but I couldn't trust myself to talk. I kept thinking that Ace must have been right here in town all the time or he couldn't have arrived as fast as he had. And if he'd been in town, he could have stopped everything that had happened. Father would still be whole and well; Pegleg would still be alive.

I mounted my horse and rode to Doc Trego's house. Anne was sitting on the porch swing. I tied my horse to the hitching post, an iron one with a lion's head for a top, and walked up to the porch. "How is he?"

"Resting now. What happened over in town? I heard some shots."

"Paul shot Pegleg and killed him."

"Dane, how awful! How . . .?"

I interrupted harshly. "I don't know what's going on, so don't ask me. All I know is that Paul was foreclosing on Pegleg. Pegleg came into town loaded for bear. He fought with Father and then went up to Paul's office. He pulled his gun and while he was grappling with Paul it went off."

Anne's face was shocked, I sat down on the porch steps and buried my face in my hands. Pegleg's death was hard to accept. It was difficult to realize that he was gone.

I shook off my morbid thoughts as Doc Trego came out on the porch. I asked, "How is he?"

Doc's face was angry. "Damn it, I told him this would happen if he didn't control that stinking temper of his!"

"Doc . . ."

"All right. All right! He's crippled, that's how he is. He'll probably never walk again. There's some paralysis along his whole left side, but part of it will pass. He'll be able to talk in about a week. In a month, he'll probably be able to use both hands. But he'll never walk again."

"You're sure?"

He looked at me pityingly. "Nothing is sure in this world. You ought to know that." He turned angrily and stamped back into the house.

Anne smiled at me apologetically. "Don't mind him. He gets this way when people won't take his advice and then suffer for it."

A feeling of hopeless discouragement began to come over me, but behind it a smoldering anger was stirring. I didn't know what was going on, but whatever it was, it was sinister and dangerous. I knew what the consequences of Father's stroke would be. Every man within a hundred miles who had a grievance against Sunblade would figure that now was the time to get even. Sunblade's strength had been no greater than the strength of John Sunblade. Now, that strength was gone forever.

I looked at Anne. Her eyes were soft and bright with tears. "I'm sorry, Dane. I'm awfully sorry."

"Thanks." I felt as though a load had been placed on my shoulders, I knew that if Sunblade survived, I must be the one who held it together. Neil would be no help. Nor would Tom.

I said, "Anne, I've been courting you ever since we were kids. Marry me — now — today. I'll never need you more than I do right now."

For an instant her eyes were startled. Then she shook her head. "It wouldn't work, Dane. Your father is going to be impossible to live with for a long, long time. He'll be fighting his helplessness, and he'll strike out at everyone within range. Not that I couldn't take that. But you'd spend more time defending me against him than you would fighting for Sunblade."

"We could live in town."

She shook her head. "Dane, you know that wouldn't work. You'd kill yourself riding back and forth to be with me. No, Dane, I can't marry you now. I won't make things more difficult for you than they already are."

It was the wrong time and the wrong way to propose to a girl. I knew that. But the knowledge only made the wound of her refusal pain the more.

Anne was on the swing; I was on the steps. The distance between us might as well have been a hundred miles. I stared at her coldly, and a little flush was born in her face. I got to my feet.

"I suppose Doc wants Pa to stay here a while."

"Yes." Her voice was almost inaudible. Her great, dark eyes were stricken.

I deliberately looked away. "Then I'll be going. Have Doc send word when Pa can come home and I'll send for him."

She didn't reply. I stalked down the path and untied my horse. I didn't even look back.

I felt the impulse to turn, to run back and take her in my arms. But I didn't. I set my jaw, mounted and rode away.

Pete Hanley saw me coming from the bench in front of the Ashlock Hotel. He was mounted by the time I reached him, and he fell in beside me. He started to say something, but after a look at my face, remained silent.

We rode for nearly five miles before he finally spoke. He said. "It's on you now, Dane. It's all on you."

I looked at him irritably. "You think I don't know that?"

He reached over and gripped my knee. "You'll make it. You always have."

I grinned at him sheepishly. "Pete, did you ever want to hit somebody — anybody — for no good reason at all?"

He nodded. "Hang onto that feeling. Give 'em a week, an' there'll be plenty of targets for you. They've been waiting for this — every rag-tag nester and greasy-sack cowman for a hundred miles."

"How will they hit us? Cattle? Or land?"

He grinned. "Ever watch coyotes pull down a beef? They're pretty damn cautious at first until they find out how much strength is left in the critter they're after. That's the way they'll be with us. They'll rustle our cattle first, in small bunches, from back in the breaks where it's pretty safe. But if they make that stick . . . Well, draw your own conclusions."

"Then we'll see to it they don't make it stick. I'll put half the crew to line riding."

Pete nodded approval.

I did just that, as soon as I arrived home. But I didn't send the men out in ignorance of what had happened. I wanted them to have it straight, from me, rather than to get it second hand and perhaps exaggerated as well.

They rode out soberly, half a dozen of them. I sent Dave Franks out to gather more and put them to the same task.

Pete went over to Pegleg after Sunblade's cut from their roundup, and the next day brought them in along with our beef herd which we'd been holding for their arrival. And that same afternoon, Pete Hanley started out with the beef drive for the railroad, two hundred and twenty miles north, taking with him all that remained of our crew.

I rode out with Pete to the holding ground, and watched the herd of nearly twelve-hundred grass-fat steers slowly begin to move. There was something ponderously majestic about it, and something sobering too, for here was the Sunblade's harvest for the whole past year.

I watched until they were nothing but lifting dust on the far horizon, and then turned my horse to return to the ranch. I had never felt more alone in my life, nor had I ever felt a heavier weight of responsibility. If the wolves struck now, I'd have less than half the crew with which to fight.

The house was a great, echoing barn of a place with no one in it except myself and Neil. For almost a week I paced its monstrous living room incessantly, threading between its ponderous pieces of furniture, going to the window often to glance out across the vast and empty land.

But none of the crew came in, and gradually I began to relax. I did not realize that the crippling of John Sunblade had been as great a shock to the rest of the country as it had to me, and that it takes a while before shock begins to wear away.

A week after Father's stroke, they brought him home. Doc drove the buggy, and Paul Lasher rode beside it. Pa sat on the seat, ponderous and immovable as stone, glaring at the world from out of his brooding, angry eyes.

Doc had a wheelchair tied on the back of the buggy. I got it off and put it on the gallery. Paul and I carried Father to it and settled him in it as gently as we could. He glared at us as though we were personally responsible for his misfortune, then, using but one hand, clumsily turned himself around and wheeled himself into the house.

Inside the door, he looked around, his eyes softening not at all. He looked at me and mumbled thickly, "How're things goin'?"

"All right. Pete left for the railroad a week ago with the beef gather. The rest of the crew is riding line."

"Riding line? What the hell for?"

I met his eyes steadily, knowing somehow that if I let him cow me today I was lost. I said, "I figure with you laid up the whole damn countryside is going to try and cut a slice of Sunblade. I don't intend to let them. That's all."

He snorted. "They will like hell! They don't dare. Not while I'm alive."

I said stubbornly, "They know what's happened to you. As far as they're concerned . . ."

His face flushed, and the vein in his forehead swelled. He growled, "I might as well be dead. Is that what you mean?"

I nodded.

Paul interrupted us smoothly. "John Sunblade is a hell of a long ways from being dead. He can still hold together what he built. I think you're getting all stirred up over nothing, Dane."

I looked at him. "There are a couple of thing you've done that need explaining. Where the hell did you get $73,000 to loan Pegleg? And why the foreclosure? He could have paid it if you'd given him a little time."

Paul smiled tolerantly. "He never would have paid it — not the way he was going. He was drunk most of the time. He wouldn't attend to business. I had no choice. The lenders . . ."

I said, "Yeah. The lenders. Who were they? Father wouldn't have been one of them, would he?"

Father made a strangled sound of rage. Paul glanced at him quickly, then back to me. His expression of concern was to me sickeningly false. He said, "Doc warned against excitement. Are you trying to kill him?"

I looked at him steadily, and at last I said, "Paul, I grew up with you. You're almost like a brother to me. But I want you to get one thing straight. Work against me and I'll fight you as quick as I'd fight a stranger. Try to wreck Sunblade and I'll kill you."

He looked at my father helplessly, as if to say, "What's the matter with him? What's he talking about?"

Father didn't say anything. He was watching me with inscrutable eyes.

I turned and stamped out of the house. Doc Trego was getting ready to leave. I asked, "Anything special he needs, Doc?"

He looked down at me from the buggy seat. "He can still have another stroke if he don't say calm. So keep the ranch's troubles from him as much as you can. Maria Sanchez can take care of him all right so far as his physical needs go."

I nodded. Doc said, "You've got a fight on your hands, Dane."

I nodded. I hesitated a moment, then said, "Doc, do me a favour. Tell Anne I'm sorry."

He grinned. "I'll do that." He clucked to his buggy horse and drove away. Inside the house I could hear the drone of voices as Paul and Father talked. I wondered what they were talking about, but I was too stiff-necked to eavesdrop. Afterward I wished I had.

Paul returned to town that evening, and I resumed my pacing and waiting. Another week passed uneventfully. Then, all at once, hell broke loose.

First it was the crew that had driven the beef herd to the railroad. They returned in a body with the news that raiders had struck the herd just across the Colorado line, stampeding it. And when they had finished gathering the scattered cattle, they discovered they were two hundred short.

It had begun, then. It had really begun. At first I blamed myself for not foreseeing the strike against our herd, but I realized eventually that I could have done nothing to prevent it. If I'd sent more men with the herd, I'd have left the ranch unprotected. And then they'd have hit the ranch instead of the herd.

The important thing was, we had lost two hundred head, worth nearly eight thousand dollars. Even more important were the inevitable consequences.

Lasher rode out to the ranch and was with Father for nearly three hours. Their voices raised at times until they were almost shouting. Then they would fall until they were inaudible.

At last, Father called for me. "Send Pete Hanley in."

I called Pete and sent him in. He grinned at me ruefully as he headed for Father's office. "Goin' to give me hell for losin' those cattle, I suppose."

I waited.

It was a different Pete who came out of the office fifteen minutes later. His ruddy face was gray, his eyes smoldering with fury. He would have passed me without speaking, but I caught his arm.

"Pete, what the hell's the matter?"

He shook off my hand. "The ornery old bastard!"

"What did he do?"

"He demoted me, that's what he did. Put Dave Franks in my place as foreman."

Pete scowled at me for an instant, then stamped off toward the bunkhouse. I went into Father's office.

Father's face was almost purple. Paul Lasher was loosening his collar frantically and fanning his face. He looked at me warningly. "Don't take it up now, Dane, unless you want to kill him."

I glared at them both. Then I turned without a word and left the room.

Pete was in the bunkhouse packing his warsack when I arrived. He moved with angry finality. He ignored me as I came in to the room.

I sat down on the edge of a bunk. "What happened, Pete?"

"Just what I told you happened."

I said, "You think it's the old man's idea?"

"What the hell difference does it make whose idea it was?"

"Might make a lot. If it was Paul's idea, then things might look different."

"What are you gettin' at?"

"Paul's up to something. Johnny Dolan went to town for the mail yesterday and he said there was talk in town about Paul marrying Pegleg's widow."

Pete's eyes sharpened. "So?"

"So, if Paul owns Pegleg by foreclosure, why the rush to marry Juanita Johnson?"

"You mean she might have a claim?"

"She's got a claim. She can redeem Pegleg. But I think there's more to it than that."

"You think she knows something about the way Paul got those notes?" Pete frowned, "It's crazy. Still, if she did know something Paul could sure keep her quiet by marryin' her, couldn't he? A wife can't testify against her husband. And she'd be satisfied too. She'd have Pegleg back without having to pay off the mortgage."

I said, "It's an idea."

"But what's all that got to do with me? Why would Paul want me out as foreman?"

"Simple enough. To weaken Sunblade. I think he wants Sunblade too."

"He'll play hell getting it."

I shook my head. "Don't underestimate him. I don't know how he'll manage, but I'll bet he's got a plan."

Pete sat down on the bunk edge and rolled a smoke. I said, "Pete, don't leave. I need you here. Stay on as a cowhand, and I promise that before I'm through you'll be foreman of Sunblade again."

Still he hesitated. I was ready to use my clincher, and ask him to stay for Mother's sake. But it wasn't necessary. He grinned at me, his eyes twinkling at last.

"All right, Dane. We'll give them a fight. If they get Sunblade, we'll make them pay for it. Through the nose."

CHAPTER
TEN

The next morning I was up at daybreak. A feeling of uneasiness had been growing in me all during the past two weeks of idle waiting.

The crew was out, line riding, and I should have had nothing to worry about until I heard from them. Yet somehow, the feeling of uneasiness persisted.

I asked Pete to keep an eye on things at the ranch and rode south toward the low line of hills nearly fifteen miles away, the hills that roughly marked Sunblade's southern border.

It was early November, but the air was dry and warm, with no hint as yet of coming winter. A big buck antelope watched me curiously from a nearby knoll, and returned to his grazing when I had passed. Dry grass waved in the stiff breeze for as far as the eye could see. The hills in the distance were blue with haze.

I caught myself hurrying my horse, and deliberately slowed him down, trying to rationalize this feeling of foreboding that troubled me.

It must be uncertainty, I decided at last. It was not knowing where they would strike, or when. It was not knowing what plan lay behind Paul Lasher's devious eyes and deceptively pleasant smile.

But it was something else as well. Upon me rested responsibility for holding Sunblade, and yet I did not have complete authority to act as I saw fit. Father sat, ponderous and irascible, in his wheelchair at home and held the reins. And Paul stood behind him, sure of Father's confidence and approval.

As I rode, the sun rose higher and higher in the sky. Shortly before mid-morning, I reached the line of low hills that marked our southern boundary.

I dismounted here and rolled a cigarette. Dragging the smoke deep into my lungs, I stared out across the vast miles of Sunblade range.

Almost farther than the eye could see, it stretched, until it ended on the near slope of the rising mountains to the north. And all around it, east and west, north and south, there were little outfits, eyeing enviously the rich grassland that Sunblade claimed, comparing this with the rocky, barren slopes of their own nearly waterless range.

Nor had they any reason to like us. For twenty-five years Father had ridden this land at the head of his well-armed crew, pushing them back, threatening, over-riding their rights and wishes, sometimes buying them out when their backs showed signs of stiffening, but always expanding, always growing.

Now, unless we were ruthless and hard, the crowding process would reverse itself. They'd push down from their hilly ranges and each would seize and claim his particular coveted section of Sunblade.

In spite of the warming rays of the sun, I suddenly felt cold. A shiver ran along my spine.

Mounting again, I set out to the east, to ride our line. To quiet my crawling uneasiness, I had to be sure that nothing was amiss, that Sunblade crewmen rode our lines holding back the encroachers.

I traveled steadily until noon when I reached the tiny sod lineshack in which the two riders who covered this section of range spent their nights.

It was empty. I felt the stove and found it still slightly warm. The bunks were unmade, and clothes were scattered carelessly around the dark and tiny room. The door was ajar.

I opened a can of beans and ate them cold out of the can. I drank two cups of the lukewarm coffee on the stove. Then, mounting again, I rode out. As I rode, I studied the ground, and wondered why I did.

I hadn't expected the two line riders to be present at their shack in mid-day, but something bothered me. Perhaps it was that I had seen no sign of either man all morning. Perhaps it was that I had seen no tracks, at least had noticed none.

So now I watched carefully, and the odd, uneasy feeling began to grow.

In mid-afternoon, I suddenly came upon a trail of cattle, nearly missing them because they followed an outcropping of rocky, shaly ground that ran along the edge of a low escarpment. A pile of dung caught my eye, and made me study the ground closely. It was then that I saw the tracks.

I halted my horse and studied the ground carefully. Ten or fifteen cattle had been driven through here, I guess. One horseman had ridden in their rear, one on each side, apparently to keep them from straying off to either side of the streak of rocky ground.

Anger boiled suddenly in my mind, but I held it down and turned into the trail. I followed for nearly a mile before the rocky ground played out and the trail cut out across a soft and grassy flat.

Here I stopped again. I had hoped I would find the pursuing tracks of Sunblade's line rider. But I found nothing.

I followed for yet another mile. And then, suddenly, I found the thing I had feared I would.

There, in a tiny valley hidden by tawny hills on all four sides, I found where the cattle had been dropped. They had spread out to graze while their three drovers had stopped to talk with yet another rider.

I judged they had talked for nearly half an hour, for half a dozen wheat-straw cigarette butts littered the ground. Then the tracks of the single rider angled away, heading northeast, and the drovers gathered their stolen herd and went on.

I hesitated only a moment, and then took the trail of the single rider, knowing where the trail would lead me, and overcome with anger greater than any I had felt in a long, long time.

The trail angled back to the foot of the hills where the rolling grassland began. Thereafter, it followed our southern boundary consistently.

I lifted my six-shooter from its holster and looked at it. And I realized with a shock that for the first time in my life I wanted to kill a man. I wanted to kill that treacherous crew member, whoever he was, who could accept Sunblade's pay with one hand while he sold us out with the other.

Most disturbing of all was the doubt that kept growing in me as I rode. If one member of Sunblade's crew was in cahoots with the rustlers, others might be as well. And if I couldn't trust the crew, I was lost.

The sun began its downward journey toward the western horizon. I judged it was close to two o'clock when I topped a long rise of ground and saw a distant horseman coming toward me.

I abandoned the trail at once and rode directly toward him. Before I had gone a mile, I recognized him as Deuce Laverne.

He was a tall, wiry man with a hollow, cadaverous face and deep-set greenish eyes. There was a week's stubble of mouse-colored whiskers on his face, and a pale scar on his left cheek.

He studied me carefully as we approached each other. He must have recognized me, yet his face showed no signs of it until he was a hundred feet away. Then he said, his voice hoarse, "Hello, Dane. How's the old man?"

I eyed him coldly. "No change." I rode around behind him and looked at the tracks his horse had made. I swung to face him. "You dirty pup! I ought to kill you! I ought to blow your damned treacherous head off!"

"What the hell are you talkin' about anyway? What's got into you?"

I stared at him furiously. His eyes shifted. His hand inched along his dusty thigh. He must have touched his horse lightly with boot or spur on the side away from me, for the animal swiveled slightly, hiding Deuce's whole right side.

I knew in an instant his hand would go for his gun. I was pretty sure I could beat him to it, but suddenly I wanted more than that. I wanted to know who the three drovers were that he'd met in that tiny valley. I wanted their hides too.

I dug my spurs savagely into my horse's flank, and the startled animal lunged ahead. Yanking his head aside, I drove him straight into Deuce's mount.

My elbow caught Deuce in the throat. Choking, he dragged his gun from its holster and tried to bring it around. I slashed him across the face with the ends of my reins.

Blinded, he fired, but the gun wasn't even pointing at me. At its sound, both horses jumped. Deuce's horse began to buck, but I yanked up the head of mine and held him still. Deuce piled over the horse's rump and the horse galloped away, I hit the ground running. Deuce had lost his gun as he fell, and now he dived for it.

I intercepted him and kicked. My boot struck his right arm just below the elbow and he howled involuntarily with pain. He tried to pick up the gun with his left hand, but I kicked it away. My voice was strange to my ears as I said, "Who were the three men you met back there? Talk, or I'll bust you wide open!"

He struggled to his feet. He turned his back on me deliberately and walked toward his hat where it lay on the ground ten feet away. Furious, I lunged at him.

100

Suddenly, he turned, and I knew, too late, why he had turned his back. In his hand he held his cartridge belt, by buckle and end. The middle of it, filled with .44 cartridges, swung at my head like a weighted club.

I tried to duck, but was caught off guard. The belt and cartridges struck me on the ear and flung me aside.

My head rang. The ear felt as though it had been torn from my head. I could feel wet blood running along my jaw and down my neck.

He was after me like a panther, using the belt like a whip. The first blow struck my shoulder as I rolled, the second nearly broke my back. The third, catching me as I rose, struck squarely on the top of my head.

It drove me back down. On hands and knees, groggy and almost out, I dropped my head as though to protect it from the next slashing blow. But as it fell, I rolled deliberately onto my back and grabbed frantically for the whistling belt.

Only the fact that it looped as it swung saved me. I could never have closed my hand on it. But it hooked on my wrist, and I crooked my elbow to hold it.

Its force, so suddenly halted, yanked it from Deuce's hand. He piled down on top of me, trying to recover it, and we rolled briefly on the ground, kneeing, clawing.

He got the belt end in both hands and held on. I surged to my feet and yanked it away.

Standing a little hunched, labouring for breath, I shook my head, trying to clear the numbness from it. Deuce blurred before my eyes.

He scrambled along the ground on all fours and grabbed at something half hidden in the grass. I saw what it was as he brought it up. His gun.

Holding the belt by the buckle end, I swung it, whistling around my head and rushed at him. An instant before the gun roared, the swinging belt struck it away.

Then I got both ends of the belt in my right hand and began to whip Deuce with it. Panting, sweating, growling curses I clubbed him on the head, the shoulders. He tried to rise and I kneed him in the face. He doubled up to protect his belly, and suddenly the gun belt wasn't enough to satisfy me. I flung it away, dived at him and began to rain my fists down into his face and throat and chest.

Only when his body went limp and unresisting, did I stop. I got up angrily, still unsatisfied. I recovered my gun which had fallen from its holster during the struggle. I found Deuce's gun and flung it as far away as I could into the high grass.

I rolled a cigarette with trembling hands. I felt drained and weak. The intensity of my own fury a few moments before frightened me. I sat down on the ground and dragged smoke deep into my lungs.

Deuce groaned, but he didn't move. His cheek was laid open clear to the bone, and blood welled thickly from the two-inch cut. I thought furiously, "Now you'll have another scar to remember Sunblade by."

When my knees stopped shaking, I got up. My horse was grazing fifty feet away. I caught him, rode a couple of hundred yards and caught Deuce's horse. Then I returned, but I did not dismount.

Deuce was conscious now, trying to sit up. I watched him fail twice, feeling no pity, nothing at all but the smoldering hatred I had felt before the fight. I looked down and asked, "Who were they?"

He looked at me blankly.

I said harshly, "Damn you, talk! And talk fast, or I'll load you up and take you back to Sunblade. I'll hang you right there in the yard for the rest of the crew to see."

He looked up. He tried to talk but words wouldn't come. He licked his battered lips, cleared his throat and finally managed, "What if I do talk?"

"Then I'll give you twenty-four hours to get out of the country."

"A horse?"

"No. This is a Sunblade horse. You walk."

He stared at me steadily for a long minute, looking, no doubt, for some sign of relenting in me. He found none, and finally he said, "All right. It was Ed Slaughter and them two young kids of his."

I had suspected as much. Slaughter's place was one of three that bordered Sunblade on the south.

I said, "Stop by Slaughter's place on your way out of the country. Tell Ed to deliver that bunch of cattle he took to Sunblade within forty-eight hours or I'm coming after him. And if I ever see you again, I'll kill you on sight. Understand?"

He nodded, his eyes smoldering. I turned my back and rode away, trailing the horse he'd been riding, behind me. I looked back from the crest of the next rise and saw him limping south toward the tawny, rolling hills.

CHAPTER
ELEVEN

I was fully aware, even as I rode away, that Deuce Laverne should never have been allowed to live. Making a merciless example of him would probably have discouraged others like him who were entertaining the same notion he'd had that they could steal from Sunblade now with impunity. Father would have dragged him home at the end of a rope and hanged what was left of him from the massive crossarm over the corral gate.

I shrugged painfully, wondering which of us, Deuce or myself, had taken the worst beating this afternoon. There was a lump on the top of my head as big as a walnut. My ear was still bleeding. My back and shoulders were stiff and sore.

And that afternoon, for the first time, I began to doubt my ability to hold on. If Deuce had been in with the rustlers, it was possible, even likely, that others of our crew were in with them too, or were rustling on their own.

Father had inspired no loyalty in the men who worked for him; he had only ruled by fear. Pete Hanley, I decided, and possibly Johnny Dolan, were the only ones I could really rely on. Three men couldn't hold more than half a million acres of grassland and ten thousand cattle by themselves.

I shrugged. The thing was done. I'd know soon enough how serious a mistake I'd made. If Ed Slaughter showed up with the stolen cattle, well and good. If he didn't, then I'd have to make good my word and go after him.

I'd gone half a dozen miles when I saw in the distance a pond Father had dredged out years before to collect the sporadic flow of Squaw Creek for stock water. Suddenly, looking at its clean, shimmering surface, I wanted to ride to it and plunge in as I had so many times before when I was a boy. I reined over, and ten minutes later dismounted beside the pond.

It was surrounded by cottonwoods. One of them had a low limb that projected out over the water. The bark on top of the limb was worn smooth by bare feet — mine and my brothers'. We'd used to climb that tree, walk along the almost horizontal limb, and dive from it into the water.

Grinning reminiscently, I shucked out of my clothes, climbed the tree, walked out on the limb, and dove in.

The water was cold, icy cold, and I came to the surface gasping. I paddled furiously for a few moments, then swam ashore, and, emerging on the bank, shook myself like a dog.

Paul, Tom, Neil and myself had not been the only ones who had used the pond, I remembered. Chiquita Johnson used to come here too. And Rosalia Sanchez, Maria's daughter. And sometimes Anne Trego with a bunch of the kids from town.

As soon as I was dry, I put on my underwear and pants and sat down to roll a smoke and put on my boots. Suddenly there was a splash across the pond, a splash that startled me and made me reach instinctively for my holstered gun on the ground nearby.

Then my hand dropped away and, grinning, I watched the bobbing head cross the pond toward me. I finished pulling on my boots as she walked out of the water, dripping, shivering, her teeth chattering with the cold.

It was Chiquita Johnson, filled out startlingly since I'd last seen her. She wore a thin cotton shift that came to her knees and, obviously, nothing under it. It clung to her body revealingly.

She shook out her wet hair, bending forward. Droplets showered me. Laughing, shivering, she straightened. "My God, that's cold! How'm I ever going to get warm again?"

Her eyes were mocking, but there was an underlying quality of seriousness about them, and I knew what she was getting at. I said, "Lie down in the sun, why don't you."

I was shivering almost as badly as she was, but not from the cold. She stretched herself out beside me and let the sun beat down on her. After a moment she murmured "Mmmmm. This is nice."

I leaned toward her, then pulled back. My voice was hoarse. "You come here often?"

She opened her eyes and regarded me sleepily. She nodded slightly. "Whenever I can."

I said, "I'm sorry about Pegleg. I tried . . ."

"I know. I heard." Her eyes glistened.

I made another cigarette with trembling hands. I lighted it and dragged smoke into my lungs. Chiquita sat up. "Give me a puff."

I held it to her lips. She took a puff. She blew the smoke straight into my face.

Suddenly she was tight in my arms, and not cold at all. Her body burned against me. I kissed her, and I felt like I was drowning.

I know now that Chiquita was not nearly so inexperienced that day as I, but it seemed then that we explored the mysteries of lovemaking together. When we were through and lay spent and warm in the late afternoon sun, the troubles that had harried me so long seemed suddenly lighter. I felt more confidence than I had before in my ability to hold things together.

I lay there staring at the drifting clouds in the sky, and suddenly I became aware that Chiquita was crying softly beside me.

I drew her to me. Her wet hair lay against my face "What's the matter? Are you sorry?"

She shook her head. "It isn't that, Dane. It's . . . just everything, I guess. Father dying — and now Mother's going to marry that damn Paul Lasher."

I sat up. "Already?"

Her eyes were angry. "She's been sleeping with him for months."

"Did Pegleg know?"

She shrugged. "I don't know. I don't see how he could have helped knowing. Paul wasn't the first one by any means."

108

"Was that what started him drinking?"

She shook her head. "I don't think so. I think your father did that to him years ago over that nester business when he took ten of Dad's cattle."

I remembered that guiltily, because what had happened that day was partly my fault. If I hadn't tried to save those nesters . . .

I changed the subject abruptly. "What do you know about the mortgage — the notes Pegleg gave Paul?"

She shook her head. "Not very much. I just don't see how he could have gotten in that deep. And I don't know where Paul could have got that kind of money unless he got it from your father."

I rolled another smoke. Chiquita reached for the sack and made one for herself as expertly as a man.

She looked out at the pond. "God, I dread swimming back in that cold water."

I grinned. "I'll get your stuff." I went to my horse, mounted and rode around the pond. Her horse was tied to a tree near the bush on which she'd hung her clothes. I gathered up her clothes, then untied the horse and led him back around the pond. I tied him, then carried her clothes to her. I watched her put them on, confused and puzzled by my own emotions. I didn't love her, didn't want to marry her. And yet I felt a protective tenderness toward her I'd never felt for anyone else but Anne.

Thinking of Anne brought a feeling of guilt to my mind. I helped Chiquita up to her sidesaddle. As she rose to it, she brushed my face with her lips. "Goodbye, Dane. If your family was all like you . . ."

I was glad to see her go. The guilt had begun to grow in me in spite of myself. Damn it, if only Anne had married me . . .

I picked up the reins of Deuce's horse and kicked mine into a run, as though the wind rushing past my face could clear my thoughts. But my thoughts went on.

There was only one way Pete Hanley and I could win this fight, I decided. It was to discharge every Sunblade rider that either of us suspected of disloyalty. One of us should ride down into Arizona and hire a crew of gunfighters. Then maybe we could hold Sunblade in spite of the odds against us. I made up my mind that as soon as I got home I'd see if something couldn't be done to make it possible.

But when I returned, there were other developments that put it temporarily from my mind. Father saw me ride in from his wheelchair on the porch and beckoned peremptorily.

I walked over to him. He asked, "What the hell happened to you?"

"I had a fight with Deuce Laverne."

"What about?"

"He was in cahoots with Ed Slaughter to steal some steers."

"You kill him, boy?"

I said "I beat him up and sent him to Ed Slaughter afoot to tell him to bring back the steers. I told him if I ever saw him again I'd kill him."

Father shook his head pityingly. It angered me, but I didn't say anything. He said, "Well, Pegleg's been thrown in with Sunblade. We've got both crews to fight with."

My anger increased. "What good is that going to do? You think Pegleg's crew is loyal to us? You think our own crew is?"

"They'd better be."

"What if they're all like Deuce? What are you going to do?"

His face began to mottle. I said, "What we need is a dozen gunfighters. Somebody we can count on."

He snorted savagely. I said, "I can send Pete Hanley south to hire them. He can be back in two weeks."

"No."

"Why not, damn it?"

"Don't argue with me. We've got plenty of crew. If you had any sand . . ."

The vein was pulsing in his forehead. His hands on the arms of his wheelchair trembled. I shrugged, stifling my anger with an effort. "All right. I'll do the best I can with what we've got."

I was puzzled about the throwing together of the two ranches, and wondered how Paul would fit into the new setup. I asked, "If Pegleg and Sunblade have been thrown in together, then Paul . . ."

He interrupted harshly, "Paul's in charge, next to me. You handle the ranch work; we'll handle the rest."

I looked at his face. It was hard as granite. Arguing with him would have been like throwing cow chips at a stone wall.

I walked away, and he shouted angrily after me, "When I was on my feet we didn't need any damn gunfighters! We wouldn't need any now if you . . ." But I was out of earshot and didn't hear the rest.

Pete was in the bunkhouse, smoking and reading an old newspaper. He looked up as I came in. I asked, "Pete, how many of the Sunblade crew can we count on?"

He frowned. "Johnny Dolan. Maybe a couple of others, maybe more. I'd say five or six at the most."

"Then we'd better call 'em in and put them to scouting our boundaries. Ed Slaughter and those two boys of his have got one bunch of our stuff that I know of. Deuce Laverne was in cahoots with 'em. I sent him to Slaughter to tell him if he didn't drive the stuff in here before forty-eight hours was up, I was coming after them."

Pete said, "I'll get on it." He got up and went out and a few moments later I heard him ride out. He'd ride all night, I knew, and by tomorrow there would be men we could trust checking our boundaries for the tracks of cattle moving off our range.

I was relieved, but I knew it was only a temporary relief. We could do little to stop piecemeal rustling with only half a dozen men.

At sundown, a buggy drove in, carrying Paul, dressed in a fancy broadcloth suit, and Juanita Johnson, dressed in a wedding gown. Tin cans bumped along behind the buggy, and there was loose rice on the floorboards. They were both half drunk, and hilariously noisy.

Paul carried her into the house and went looking for a bottle. Pa sat looking on, grinning lecherously.

I congratulated them both half-heartedly and then stamped angrily out of the house. If I had doubted before that Pa had been part of the plan for ruining Pegleg, I doubted it no longer.

Looking around in the early dusk, I wondered why I was letting myself get so damn sweated up over holding onto Sunblade. What did it matter to me? I'd be better off if I rode away without even bothering to look back. I could marry Anne and we could go to any of a hundred places and be happy together. I could make my way.

And yet, there was more to Sunblade than an old man chained to his wheelchair nursing his voracious greed. There was definitely something about it that human indecency couldn't hurt.

Memories of growing up, of my mother and of my father, too, in the years before she went away. The endless, brooding miles of grass, every inch of which I knew. The way it looked when snow drove across it from the north, when spring brought the grass up, greening underfoot.

And there was something else as well. There was a promise I had made in Denver several years before, a promise made to my mother just before she died.

No. I'd go on. In spite of Father, in spite of Paul, I'd fight for Sunblade. I'd fight, and in the end, the good Lord willing, I'd win.

CHAPTER
TWELVE

At the end of forty-eight hours, there was still no sign of Ed Slaughter, his two sons, or the bunch of Sunblade cattle they had stolen. The time had come either for me to hand the country an example, or start running.

At dawn of the following day, I walked from the house to the bunkhouse to get Pete Hanley. Dave Franks was also there.

I said, "Dave — Pete — I want to talk to you."

Franks scowled, but he followed Pete and me out the door into the chill wind that blew from the north. Overhead a thin layer of clouds had spread, and now drove along, visibly swift, toward the south.

I said, "I gave Ed Slaughter a deadline to return those cows he stole. Now it's time to do something about it."

Franks said, "Well, I don't know. I'll have to see either Paul or your old man . . ."

I said, "You'll have to see no one. Go saddle a horse and be ready to leave in ten minutes."

His face flushed. He stared at me rebelliously. But in the end he dropped his glance and followed Pete.

Ten minutes later we rode out. It was cool, and we could push the horses pretty hard, so we reached Sunblade's southern line around mid-morning.

Pete hauled his horse to a halt and hipped around in the saddle. "How we goin' to work this? We'd better not ride straight in. No tellin' how many Slaughter's got with him."

I grinned, to hide my inner uncertainty. I said, "I don't give a damn how many are with him. We're riding straight in by the road, just as though we had fifty men at our backs."

Franks growled, "The hell with that! They'll cut us down."

I looked at him steadily. "I don't know how solid you are with Paul, or with the old man either. But I can tell you one thing for sure. You won't be foreman if you weasel out on this. The old man will stand for a lot, but he won't stand for that. Now make up your mind. Ride with us or ride on back."

I watched the play of doubt and uncertainty on his face. Pete, watching too, began to grin. Franks saw the grin and his face reddened. I turned and rode out, with Pete Hanley close behind. Franks hesitated an instant, looked once toward Sunblade, then followed.

We hit the two-track road leading to Slaughter's place about ten minutes later. It climbed steadily in the rising hills, washed out in places, filled in spots so that a wagon could get through. It was almost noon when we came through a slot in a saddle-shaped hill and could look down on it.

The house, a sagging one-room shack, was built of logs, chinked with a mixture of manure and mud. It had a sod roof from which a profusion of weeds had grown. Now they were as brown and dry as the grass underfoot.

Besides the house, there was a pole corral, and a ramshackel barn built of rough-sawed lumber which was now grayed from weather. The corral held perhaps thirty head of cattle, triple-wintered steers that Slaughter was apparently holding to throw in with his neighbors' stock when they came past on their way to the railroad. I guessed that it probably represented his beef roundup for the year.

Pete rode beside me, but Franks held back, riding behind us both.

From fifty feet, I hailed the house. "Slaughter! Come out here!"

The door opened, and Ed Slaughter stepped out. He was a tall man, gaunted and stooped. His face was seamed with deep wrinkles, and those around his mouth, downturning and hard, matched for toughness the cold gleam of his slitted eyes. His face was covered with a week's growth of reddish whiskers. He wore a dirty flannel shirt and a pair of bib overalls. On his feet were a pair of ill-fitting worn-out boots. From one of the boots a sockless toe protruded through a slit in the leather.

He stopped ten feet from the door, in a spot dampened and whitened by countless pans of soapy dishwater.

I said, "Deuce give you my message?"

He stared at me warily without answering. I could feel anger pulling at me. I swung to the ground, walked over to him and slapped him, hard, on the side of the face. I said, "Don't dummy up on me, you damned thief! Answer me! Did Deuce give you my message?"

He nodded surlily, hating me with his tiny, slitted eyes. Then he shifted his glance to the shack.

I said, "If they start shooting, it won't help you. Better tell 'em that."

He swung his head again and called in a high, cracked voice, "Keep your fingers off your triggers, boys."

I said, "All right. Head for the corral."

He was scared now. His face was pasty, his eyes flat. "What you goin' to do?"

"You'll see." I turned to Pete. "Build a fire, Pete. Scout around and find a couple of branding irons."

I turned, got on my horse and took down my rope. I dropped the loop over Slaughter's head, then yanked it tight so that it pinned his arms to his sides. He fought it for a moment, so I yanked him off his feet. When he got up, he walked along quietly until he reached the corral.

I could imagine his two sons back there in the house, and how they would be taking this. They'd want to shoot so bad they could taste it. But they'd know that if they did, their father wouldn't live a minute after the first shot was fired.

I threw the rope-end to Dave Franks. "Tie him to the corral fence."

Franks dismounted and did as he was told. Pete had found some branding irons in the barn. Now he was gathering wood to start a fire. When it was going good, he laid the irons in it.

I said, "Ed, we're going to vent your brand on fifteen head of these steers and put the Sunblade brand on them. Then we're going to drive them all the way to Ashlock."

Ed swallowed, his Adam's apple bobbing. He said in a tight voice, "Dane, I'll starve. That's half my year's gather."

I said, "You've got the money for the Sunblade steers you stole. Maybe not as much as you'd have got for your own, but that's your problem, not mine."

I turned to Pete and Franks. "Let's get going. You two rope. I'll brand."

Pete dropped his loop over a steer's head. Franks caught the same steer by his hind feet. The rest of the cattle crowded away from them, bunching against the pole fence on the far side.

Pete and Franks backed their horses in opposite directions tightening their ropes and stretching the steer out. He hit the ground with a solid thump.

I took a nearly red-hot iron from the fire. First I vented Slaughter's S Bar on the big animal's hip. Then I got a fresh iron and traced the Circle-Scimitar Sunblade brand on his ribs.

I squatted on his head, holding him with a knee and one hand, while I loosened and flipped off Pete's loop. Franks slacked his rope and flipped the loop off the steer's feet expertly without dismounting.

I jumped back, letting the steer rise. He glared at me, head lowered, for an instant, then turned and trotted calmly into the bunch.

118

And so it went. An hour later we had fifteen head of Slaughter's steers vented and branded. Ed Slaughter was gray and sick-looking.

I opened the corral gate. "All right, Pete. Cut 'em out."

Pete rode into the bunch, cutting out first one and then another of the freshly branded steers. One by one, they thundered through the gate, spreading and scattering immediately.

When they were all outside, I said, "Pete, you help Franks gather 'em and start them off toward home. I'll wait until you're clear."

I squatted and rolled a smoke. Pete and Franks gathered up the scattered steers and started them out at a steady trot along the road.

I let them pass through the saddle before I moved. Then I untied Slaughter from the fence. I drew my gun and, leading my horse, prodded him around the corral until it was between me and the shack.

I said, "We've got the steers, Ed. But we can still come back and shoot up the place if you want it that way. How's it going to be?"

He studied my face furiously. What he saw in it must have told him I meant exactly what I said. He yelled at the house, "No shooting, boys! Let 'im go."

I said, "Now you're getting smart. See that you stay smart. Don't help yourself to any more Sunblade steers. Because next time it's going to cost you more than fifteen head of your own."

He didn't reply. I mounted and rode after Pete and Franks without looking back. I tried to appear confident and contemptuous but inside I was scared as hell. A spot between my shoulderblades ached in anticipation of the rifle bullet that would smash into it. But no shot came and a few moments later I had passed through the saddle of the hill and was out of sight.

What Slaughter would do now was anybody's guess. Maybe he'd come after us. Whatever he did, he'd think twice before he stole any more Sunblade cattle . . .

We drove leisurely, and corralled the cattle at Sunblade just after dark. I went in and told Father what we'd done. He nodded, but otherwise had nothing to say. I didn't know whether he approved or not.

I was tired and needed sleep. But sleep tonight was a luxury I couldn't afford. Neither Slaughter nor any of the other two-bit ranchers that encircled us could afford to let those fifteen steers reach Ashlock. Because if they did, half the wolves that were preying on us or considering it would be scared off.

So I spent the night sleeplessly sitting out beside the corral, a rifle on my knees. No one came. At dawn, red-eyed and feeling as though I'd ridden a thousand miles in the last two days, I started out for Ashlock with Franks, and Pete.

Word of what I'd done would get around the country fast enough anyway. But if I drove these cattle down the Main Street of Ashlock those who might be preying on Sunblade or considering it would have visual evidence that we would retaliate swiftly. They would know that Sunblade was neither helpless nor without direction.

120

We drove down Main. In front of Sheriff Wines' office I sent Pete Hanley ahead and we bunched the fifteen wild steers right there in the street before the sheriff's office.

Easing over to his door, I reached down from my saddle, turned the knob and kicked it open. "Ace, come here a minute."

He was already watching from the window, but now he came to the door. I said, "Take a look at the brands, Ace. These are Slaughter steers, or were. He stole some from us, so we took some of his to replace our loss. Any objections?"

Ace looked up at me. There was anger in his eyes. I had him on a spot and he knew it. If he raised no objections, it would cost him several hundred votes in the next election. If he did object, it would lose him the support of Sunblade.

He said snappishly, "Get 'em to hell out of town before somebody gets hurt."

I pushed him a little. "Then you don't object?"

He slammed the door without answering. The sudden noise stampeded the cattle and they thundered down the street and out of town. The pounding of their hoofs made windows rattle in the stores. People came into the street to stare after them.

I said, "Take 'em home, Pete," and he and Dave Franks galloped in their dusty wake.

I reined my horse over to the Ashlock Bar, then changed my mind and went on down the street toward Dutch's Place. I swung stiffly from the saddle and batted accumulated dust from my pants legs and jacket sleeves. I looped the reins over the rail and went inside.

It was a chill, raw morning and I felt it, so I walked over to the pot-bellied stove that sat between door and bar and spread my hands toward its warmth.

My glance roved down the bar, noting the way the eyes of those who had been watching me shifted. At the end of the bar a familiar figure stood, and for some reason, because I was tired and discouraged perhaps, resentment rose in me the minute I saw him.

Tom had grown like a weed in the last few years but he looked no more like Father than a deadly, dainty derringer looks like a heavy Colt .44. His dark eyes rested on me briefly, holding recklessness and rebellion and defiant mockery. He tossed off his drink and then stretched like a cat. Grinning, he came toward me, and my resentment increased.

He sauntered over to the stove, his grin carrying an open dare. "What're you doin' in town?"

I said, "A couple of things. One to show the town that nobody steals from Sunblade and gets away with it."

"What's the other?"

His mocking grin suddenly got under my hide. I said, "To bring you home. You can help."

"The old man send you to tell me that?"

"No, but I'm telling you anyway."

Tom's grin suddenly grew strained, but his glance didn't drop. He said softly, "You can go straight to hell. Now get out of here and leave me alone!"

CHAPTER
THIRTEEN

Anger flooded through me but I kept my voice even and low so that it would not carry as far as the bar. "Tom, Sunblade's backed against the wall, whether you know it or not. The old man's crippled and can't ride. Neil handles the paperwork, so he's doing his share. But I need help. Right now I'm dead for sleep and there's a thousand things I ought to be doing. Slaughter's not the only one who's been helping himself to Sunblade stock."

His look said plainly, *What the hell is that to me?*

I said, "The money you throw around so free and easy comes from Sunblade, in case you've forgotten. It's time you did something to help earn it. You've been spending your time in town, with liquor to keep you warm daytimes and a woman at night. You've had cards and dice and company to keep you amused. Maybe the old man is kind of proud to have one son that's a heller, and maybe he won't make you work. Maybe he'll dole out all the money you want as long as you're willing to swallow your pride and go asking for it. But the old man's tied to a wheelchair and it's time you carried your share of the load. I'm staying in town tonight. I'm going to have a bath and see Anne and then sleep for twelve hours. You're going back to the ranch and help run things. For a start, you're going to catch Pete and Franks and help them take that bunch of Slaughter's cattle home."

The grin had now left Tom's face entirely. He said surlily, "They don't need my help for that."

"Maybe they don't, but you're going, just the same."

Tom's eyes flashed angrily. He stuck his face close to mine. It held all the accumulated resentment of years. "Go nurse your damned cows by yourself! I'm fed up — with Sunblade — with going to the old man for every penny I need, with being bawled out like a kid every time I do something somebody doesn't like. You go straight to hell!"

I swung on him furiously, and the sound of my fist striking his jaw was like a cleaver biting through flesh and bone into a meat block beneath. He sagged and I caught him as he fell. I'd hit him harder than I intended, but there was no use worrying about that now.

I stopped a little to get under his limp body, then rose with him across my shoulder. I stamped out through the door, a little sorry for what I'd started and doubtful about how much good it would do.

Outside, I slung him across my saddle and led the horse to the livery stable down at the edge of town. From the dozen or so horses that Sunblade always kept there I saddled one for Tom. I laid him across it and loosened his belt, hooked it over the horn to hold him in place. Then, mounting my own horse, I led Tom's out of town. It had begun to snow and the flakes melted as soon as they touched the ground.

Catching the slow-moving herd, I handed the reins of Tom's horse to Franks. "He's going home with you. See that he doesn't fall off."

Franks nodded noncommittally, and I headed back toward town. There was no anticipation left in me now. There was just a sour taste in my mouth and the numbing weariness.

From things that happened later, I was able to reconstruct just about what happened between Tom and Dave Franks that day as they rode toward Sunblade.

The snow thickened as they rode, and kept melting on the warm ground until they were riding in slippery, claylike mud. Franks probably fell behind, not wanting Pete to hear what he had to say to Tom when my brother came to.

Perhaps, on the pretext of securing Tom better, he stopped and unhooked Tom's belt from the horn. And then rode on, grinning a little and waiting for Tom to recover consciousness, knowing that when he did, his sudden movement would land him on his face in the mud.

Franks was a scrawny man, sallow and unhealthy-looking, with bulbous, slightly protruding eyes. Father had never liked him, nor had I, in spite of his complete knowledge of the cattle business. Replacing Pete with Franks as foreman puzzled me. Paul must have put a hell of a lot of pressure on Pa to get it done.

When Tom groaned and stirred, the horse, feeling the unaccustomed movement from its hitherto inert burden, started and shied to one side, exactly as Franks had known he would.

Tom flopped to the ground. Rolling, grumbling curses, he scrambled to his knees, to find himself in soft, slick mud.

As Franks dismounted, he got to his feet, wiping his hands angrily on the legs of his pants. "What the hell am I doin' 'way out here?"

"Dane fetched you. You an' him had a fight, looks like."

Tom scowled bitterly. "You couldn't call it a fight." He cursed softly and steadily.

Franks murmured with fawning sympathy, "Nobody ought to have to take that — even from his brother. It ain't right."

"By God, I'm not going to take it!"

"What're you going to do?"

Tom said, "Damned if I know, but I'll sure as hell think of something."

Franks said, "If you had some money you could get out of this damn country and start over someplace else."

"Where'd I get any money? The old man doles it out a couple of twenties at a time and I have to ride out and ask for that."

Franks hesitated, studying Tom. "There are a lot of cattle on this place and Dane can't be everywhere at once. Everybody else is getting theirs. You'd just as well get your share too."

126

Tom laughed scornfully. "Where would you sell Sunblade cattle? Who'd buy 'em?"

"From a Sunblade? Anybody would. I could find a buyer in a minute."

Anger raised belatedly in Tom. He grabbed Franks by the shirtfront and yanked him close. "You sneaky son-of-a-bitch! I ought to tell the old man about this!"

Franks shrugged. "Go ahead. There's plenty of other jobs around."

Tom swung onto his horse. He spurred out along the beaten, muddy trail of the cattle, his back stiff with anger. Franks followed more leisurely, confident and unworried . . .

I rode into town by the street on which Anne Trego lived. I wanted to see her and talk to her, and yet somehow I had the feeling it would be no good. It wasn't fair to ask her to marry me and come to Sunblade now. Yet I knew things would not always be as they now were.

Wearing a coat, she came out of the door as I approached. Her lips were smiling; her eyes were soft. She unhooked the gate latch, opened the gate and came out to the edge of the street, blinking a little against the soft flakes of snow driving into her face. She said, "What was that all about?"

I dismounted. She began to walk toward Main Street and I paced beside her, leading my horse. "You saw me leave town with Tom?"

She nodded. I grinned down at her. The turmoil inside of me had quieted, and my utter weariness had become a kind of pleasant lethargy.

"I just figured it was time Tom took on part of the responsibility for Sunblade. He didn't agree."

She walked silently beside me, her face sober. I said, "Anne, sometimes you're exciting as hell. Others, you're downright soothing."

She looked at me with mocking humor lurking behind her eyes. "Which is it today?"

"Soothing," I said.

"That's a sorry kind of a left-handed compliment. A girl doesn't like to be told she's soothing."

Snow had eddied and drifted on the north sides of the houses, accumulating where the ground was not so warm. Ahead of us lay the business district of the town. I let my steps lag a little, dropping half a step behind Anne so that I could watch her. The curves of her throat and cheek were lovely.

Abruptly I said, "Anne, I want you to marry me. How long are you going to make me wait before you agree to become my wife?"

Her lips were still smiling as she turned, but some of the warmth had gone from her, and her eyes were serious, almost sad. "I don't know, Dane. I really don't. I want our marriage to have a chance, to start right and stay that way. It can't now — you know it can't. Look at you. You're so tired you can hardly stand up. You're fighting your father; you're fighting Paul and you're fighting everyone that's trying to cut themselves a piece of Sunblade. I don't want you fighting me too."

I felt my face stiffening with irritation. She laid a hand on my arm. "I'm sorry, Dane," she said.

128

I shook off her arm and mounted my horse. We had reached the corner of Main and 3rd. Across the street from us was the hotel and the Ashlock Bar. Beside us was the bank and the building containing Paul Lasher's office where Pegleg Johnson had died.

I was about to say something to Anne which I'd have regretted, but I was saved from it by Chiquita Johnson's voice, lifting excitedly from the door to the bank. "Why, Dane! How nice to see you."

I glanced at her and swung back down from my horse. I watched her cross the walk smilingly toward me. Something made me glance at Anne and I discovered she was frowning slightly.

Chiquita came straight to me and, reaching up, kissed me lightly on the mouth. Memory of the other day out by the pond, made my face flush.

Chiquita laughed at me softly, her eyes mocking. "What's the matter, Dane? You're blushing like a schoolboy."

She didn't wait for me to answer, but turned to Anne. "How are you, Anne? I haven't seen you for ages."

Anne smiled at her icily. "It has been a long time." She glanced at me, and there was hurt in her eyes. She returned her attention to Chiquita hastily. "It's nice that you and Dane can see so much of each other."

Chiquita's expression was one of exaggerated innocence. "Why, we hardly ever see each other. Do we, Dane?"

My discomfort increased. Anne, sensitive and perceptive, clearly suspected that Chiquita and I knew each other quite well.

I mumbled something about leaving, but Chiquita put out a hand and caught my arm. "Don't go. I have to hurry off anyway. Good-bye, Anne, Good-bye, Dane." She winked slyly at me and crossed the street, picking her way daintily through the mud, her skirts raised to reveal her trim ankles. For an instant Anne's eyes sparkled dangerously.

She looked at me with determined malice. "Nice, wouldn't you say?"

I tried to meet her eyes, without notable success.

"You sly dog," she said. "Have you asked her to marry you too?"

I said angrily, "Maybe I should. Maybe *she* wouldn't keep me dangling."

"No, I'd say she wouldn't. Not judging from the way she looked at you."

I said pleadingly, "Anne, for God's sake . . ."

She was contrite. "I'm sorry, Dane. Go on. Get yourself a room at the hotel and get some sleep. See me again before you leave town. Promise?"

I nodded uncomfortably. I mounted again and rode across the muddy street. As I tied my horse before the hotel, I glanced back. Anne still stood where I had left her, watching me. It was too far to tell for sure, but I thought I saw tears in her eyes.

CHAPTER
FOURTEEN

Instead of going straight into the hotel, I turned and went into the Ashlock Bar instead. A couple of drinks would not only make me sleep better, but might ease the jumpy irritability I felt. It was a new feeling to me, one I didn't like.

There were four men in the saloon. Two of them were at a table playing checkers. The other two were at the bar. Both were small ranchers from the hills on Sunblade's eastern border.

They glanced at me, nodded briefly and returned their attention to their drinks. I leaned on the bar and looked at myself in the mirror behind it.

My face was dirty and covered with two days' growth of beard. My eyes were sunk deep in their sockets.

Phil Duggan, the bartender, looked at me inquiringly. I said, "Whisky, Phil," and he slid me a bottle and glass.

He was a great, beefy man, whose bald head shone pinkly, relieved only by a slight fringe of fine black hair over his ears. His jowls and cheeks had a bluish cast from his heavy beard. He watched me pour a drink, then asked with real concern, "How's old John making

131

it? I'll bet it's hard for him in a wheelchair after all those years of doin' for himself."

I nodded, and gulped the first drink. I poured the second immediately and gulped that too. I heard the door bang shut behind me and glanced around.

Paul Lasher stood in the doorway, smiling at me. He came up beside me and nodded to Phil Duggan, who slid him a glass. He poured the glass full from the bottle in front of me and raised it to me soberly. His voice was grave, but I was struck with a feeling that behind his gravity he was pleased.

"Here's to you, Dane, for trying to make a cowman out of Tom. You can't do it, but I admire you for trying."

I scowled. "You don't miss much, do you?"

"Not if I can help it. For instance, I didn't miss that ill-advised move of yours earlier today — driving Slaughter's steers through town — flaunting them in the sheriff's face. You know, Dane, there are things that even a Sunblade can't do. You'd better begin finding out what they are."

I laughed harshly.

He frowned. "It's not funny. I had a hell of a time talking Ace out of throwing you in the jug. The man has some pride. And Tom has too. It's something you seem to forget."

I looked at him steadily. "Which side are you on? We can't hold Sunblade if we're going to think about hurting the feelings of a bunch of hungry buzzards."

His tone reproving, he said, "Does Anne fall into that category, too?"

132

I gripped the edge of the bar. "I said you didn't miss much. That was a mistake. You don't miss a damn thing!"

He smiled tolerantly. "It's my business not to miss anything, Dane."

I stared at him, trying to see behind his twinkling, half-serious eyes, his expression of false concern. He was good at verbal fencing and I wasn't. I turned and poured myself another drink.

Paul had prevailed upon Father to replace Pete Hanley, who'd been foreman for as long as I could remember, with Dave Franks, a man that neither Father nor I fully trusted. He'd married Juanita Johnson before Pegleg was hardly cold in his grave. He'd thrown Pegleg in with Sunblade, and I knew that particular act had helped us not at all so far as the rest of the country was concerned.

I suspected Paul of dishonesty in the matter of Pegleg's notes, and it wasn't beyond belief that he'd employ the same dishonesty against Sunblade . . .

I shook my head impatiently. Vague suspicions would get me nowhere. I needed something concrete.

I laid a dollar on the bar, nodded to Paul and went through the side door that led from the saloon to the hotel lobby. I got a room at the desk, took the key from the clerk, and climbed the stairs, calling back, "See that my horse gets stabled, will you?"

"Sure, Mr. Sunblade. Right away."

Inside my room, I collapsed on the bed, without even removing my boots. I closed my eyes and was instantly asleep.

Several hours later I awoke. The holstered gun at my hip was pressing cruelly into my side. Groggily I got up, removed it and hung it over one of the bedposts. I pulled off my boots and took off my clothes, except for my underwear. Then I slumped on the bed again and went back to sleep.

In the morning, there were three inches of snow on the ground. Clouds hung heavily overhead, forecasting more before the day was out.

I ate breakfast in the hotel dining room and afterward walked along to the livery stable, where I got my horse. I rode out immediately for home, wondering about Tom, refreshed by my long night's sleep.

The ranch was practically deserted, except for Father, Neil, Maria Sanchez and Rosalia, her daughter. Pete Hanley was the only one of the hands present. He was in the barn shoeing a horse. His face was flushed from the glowing forge.

He looked up as I came in, stamping the snow from my boots. I asked, "Tom stay with you all the way home yesterday?"

He nodded, grinning. "What'd you hit him with?"

"My fist. Where is he now?"

"He rode out with Dave Franks. Said they were goin' to patrol our boundaries, might be gone several days."

I stifled the vague uneasiness his answer raised in me. I asked, "Think Tom will stay with it?"

"He might. For a while. But don't expect him to change overnight, Dane."

I watched him shape a red-hot shoe expertly on the anvil, his hammer strokes clean and precise. At last I asked, "Pete, do you think that business with Slaughter's steers did any good?"

He looked at me and shrugged. "Time'll tell. Prob'aly it'll slow 'em down for a while. But this snow — well, I don't know. Looks like it might keep snowing off and on for several days. If that happens, it'll be an invitation to 'em. They can drive our stuff off and the snow'll cover their trails."

I nodded gloomily. I knew what we ought to do — what we had to do if we were going to survive. We ought to call in the crew and get rid of every one of them that we doubted. I ought to send Pete down into Arizona to gather up a fighting crew. Before the winter was out we'd need one.

At the moment I wasn't worrying about Pegleg. Let Paul and Juanita worry about that. I was damned if I was going to. I got a fresh horse out of one of the stalls, saddled and rode out.

All day I rode through the snow, thinking, watching for sign. I found nothing. And all of the following days for over a week I rode, with like results. Yet, I couldn't get rid of the uneasy feeling I had that Sunblade cattle were moving off our ranges under my very nose.

November passed, with deceptive peacefulness. The crew stayed out, riding line, and all of the reports I got from them were good — there was no rustling. And yet I knew there was.

Never had I found a trail to follow; never had I seen a stranger on our range. Maybe it was something in the faces of the crewmen; maybe it was some dogged sixth sense in me. Whatever it was, I was sure that my suspicions were well founded. Yet, with nothing to go on, I was helpless.

In early December, I decided to go into town and talk to Paul. I didn't expect him to listen to me, but I had to try. I had to convince him that we needed men we could trust.

As it turned out, the trip was for nothing. Paul was gone and his office was locked. I wandered along the street. I passed LeClair's Mercantile and stopped a moment to look into the window. Sol already had a Christmas display in the window, red and green crepe paper, toys for the kids.

Down in front of the Ashlock Bar, sitting in the sun, I noticed three strangers. They watched me steadily as I went up the steps into the store.

Strangers weren't exactly rare in Ashlock, but these three caught my eye at once, because they looked no more like drifting cowhands than a wolf looks like a shepherd dog. All wore guns and their faces held a peculiar watchfulness.

Shrugging, I entered the store. Inside, Sol LeClair stood at the gun counter, selling ammunition to two more strangers who bore the same stamp as the three I had seen outside.

Uneasiness struck me. Occasionally, of course, strangers such as these passed through town. But five of them, all at once? Something told me it was more than mere coincidence.

Occupied by my thoughts, I failed to notice Sol excuse himself and come toward me. He said, "Morning, Mr. Sunblade. What can I do for you?"

I didn't like the deference in his tone because I knew it was reserved for those who bore the Sunblade name. My voice was more abrupt than I intended. "I want some things for Christmas. I may not be in town again."

He turned and led the way toward the rear of the store, "What did you have in mind, Mr. Sunblade?"

I assumed he was through with the two strangers. Now, as I passed, one of them put a hand on my arm. "Wait a minute there, bucko. The old man was waitin' on us."

Sol swung impatiently. "I'll get back to you in a minute."

The stranger said, "You'll get back to us *now*."

I could feel anger stirring in my mind. Sol should have known better than to pull a stunt like this. It put me in an embarrassing position.

I said, "Finish with them, Sol. I can wait."

I started to step past the pair. I didn't see the boot one of them stuck in front of me, I tripped on it and sprawled to the floor. All my anger and frustration over the way things were going at the ranch boiled up in my mind.

I got up furiously, and swung a hard right that smashed into the grinning mouth of the stranger nearest to me. He staggered back, and I followed, savagely glad of something on which to vent my smoldering anger.

I swung again, and he drove back hard into a counter, smashing through its glass front.

Behind me I heard Sol yell, "Look out!" and started to turn. My eye caught a blur of movement behind me and then something exploded in my head.

It seemed no more than an instant to me before consciousness began to return. I heard voices, low-pitched and fuzzy. I struggled to open my eyes, failed for a moment, and then succeeded.

Light blinded me and I blinked against the glare from the lamp on Sol's desk. I was lying on Sol's old leather-covered sofa. There were several people standing over me, among them Doc, Sol, and Ace Wines.

The sheriff cleared his throat. "I got them two in jail, Dane. You sign this complaint an' I'll keep 'em there."

I sat up, my head pounding. "Nothing doing. Turn 'em loose."

Ace protested, "But Dane . . ."

"No." I got to my feet. Ace put a hand on my arm and I shook it off. I wanted to be outside, wanted the cold, fresh air in my nostrils. What had happened was senseless, and I wanted no more to do with it. They'd had reason enough for resenting me.

Doc was watching me sharply as I turned to go. Behind me, as I walked toward the door, I heard Ace's worried voice, "More strangers in town than I've ever seen before. I wonder why."

CHAPTER
FIFTEEN

As it turned out, I did get back into town again and so, on the twenty-third, I drove the buckboard in to buy the few things I would need, for Anne, for Father, for Maria and Rosalia.

Driving in, I passed Paul Lasher, driving his buggy toward Sunblade, but only raised a hand to wave at him and drove past without stopping. I didn't want to talk to him today.

I picked out some things in LeClair's Mercantile and afterward put them in the back of the buckboard, covering them against the softly falling snow with a small square of canvas and weighting it down with a length of chain. One small package I tucked into my sheepskin pocket, then mounted to the spring seat and took up the reins.

I headed toward Doc Trego's house, feeling a lift in my spirits for the first time in weeks, and full of excited anticipation. A buckboard whirled around the corner ahead of me, nearly colliding with me and I yanked the team to a halt. The other buckboard, filled to overflowing with laughing, shouting young people, was festooned with bells which gave off a clear, pleasant jangling.

A pretty girl, her cheeks flushed from the cold, called out, "Merry Christmas," and I waved at her. Then I went on, and pulled up in front of Doc's house, tying the team to the familiar hitching post.

I hadn't seen Anne for some time, and we'd parted last on an unpleasant note, so I was a little hesitant as I twisted the bell. But her face as she opened the door showed quick pleasure and genuine welcome. "Dane! Come in and take off your coat. Dad's out in the kitchen rushing the season, stirring up some kind of witch's brew that will either warm you or take the lining out of your stomach."

I went in and shrugged out of my coat. Anne took it from me, standing close. Her clean fragrance filled my nostrils and suddenly I reached out and caught her to me. I aimed a kiss at her lips, missed, and found her cheek instead. Anne laughed as she pulled away. "Your nose is cold. Go get a drink from Dad and let me be."

I gave her the small package. "Christmas. Maybe a kind of peace offering too."

"It was my fault, Dane. I was jealous." She changed the subject quickly. "How are things going?"

I shrugged. "All right, I guess. Nothing wrong I can put my finger on, anyway."

She carried the package to the mantel and put it there with some others. Then she left the room with my hat and coat.

I walked toward the kitchen, feeling gloomy. Anne wouldn't marry me until things had settled down, and the way things looked, they never would. I was glad to just sit in the kitchen, absorbing Doc's genial small talk and sipping the "witch's brew" he'd concocted. After a little while, Anne came to the kitchen.

"Have Christmas dinner with us, Dane. Your father will have Tom and Neil, and probably Paul as well."

Doc seconded her invitation and I nodded acceptance. "I'd like that." Then I finished my drink and rose. "I've got to be getting back. Thanks for the drink, Doc."

Anne followed me to the door and brought my coat and hat. I put them on and stood for a moment looking down at her. There were things to be said and things to be settled between us, but neither of us seemed to want to take the lead. I leaned down and kissed her on the lips, "Goodbye."

"Goodbye, Dane," she said, smiling faintly.

I left her and drove out of town at a trot. It was late afternoon now. The snow had stopped, but the sky was still heavily overcast and it seemed to be getting dark already.

I met no one until I was less than a mile from the ranch, and then I saw a horseman pounding toward me. He rode as though he were pursued by the devil, and swung off the road when he saw me coming. He passed less than a hundred feet to my right, and though he turned his head away, I recognized him as Dave Franks.

Puzzled, I went on. Had something happened at the ranch? Was Franks riding for help? But if he was, why had he so plainly avoided me? Thoroughly disturbed, I slapped the backs of the team with the reins and lifted them to a run.

A few minutes later I brought the ranch buildings into sight through the thickening darkness, startled at once by the sight of so many lamps burning there all at once. Every window in the house was lighted and there was a crowd of punchers on the gallery before the big front door. One of them had a lantern.

Without slowing, I drove directly to the house instead of to the barn as I usually did. I swung down from the seat. "What's going on? What's happened?"

The assembled punchers shuffled their boots in the snow, but none would speak. I said angrily, "Answer me, damn it! What the hell's the matter?"

Pete Hanley, having heard my arrival, came out of the big front door. He spoke to one of the men. "Put the buckboard away." Then he looked at me. "Dane — John's dead."

"Dead?" I stared at him. Shock stunned me momentarily. Saying that John Sunblade was dead was like saying the sun wouldn't rise tomorrow. But a look at Pete's face in the lantern's light told me it was true.

I pushed past him and burst into the house, with Pete following close behind. The living room was empty except for Maria and her daughter. Giving them only a glance, I swung around. "Where is he?"

"In his office. Dane . . ."

"What?"

"He was killed. Shot."

"Who did it? Damn it, who did it?"

"Dave Franks."

I strode savagely to the door. The crowd of punchers was still there, uneasy, uncomfortable. I yelled, "What the hell are you waiting for? Get after Franks, all of you. He went toward town. I want him — dead or alive! Do you understand?"

They melted into the darkness, running. I strode across the living room and onto the gallery surrounding the courtyard at the rear of the house.

The door to Father's office was open. A lamp burned on his desk amid its scattered papers. The wheelchair stood empty behind the desk. Over by the rear wall his body lay, pitifully crumpled and twisted. Directly above his head hung his Colt's .44 and cartridge belt that he'd stopped wearing when he took to the wheelchair.

From the way he lay, it was apparent that he had left the wheelchair voluntarily and crawled to the back wall. He'd tried to gain his feet and reach the gun, and he might have made it, too. But Frank's bullets had slammed him against the wall and driven the life from him.

I stared at him unbelievingly. For years there had been little or no affection between me and this embittered, hard old man, so now I could feel only a measure of sorrow. But I could feel the unreality of it, that so much raw power could be rendered impotent as abruptly as this.

Neil came into the office behind me. He was even paler than usual and his thinning hair was in disarray as though he had been running his hands through it.

He said in a low voice, "I can't believe it! I just can't believe it. Not over an hour ago I could hear him down here bellowing like a bull."

I crossed the room and slipped my arms under Father's body. He was heavy and ponderous, but in death he seemed smaller than he ever had in life. I lifted him and carried him out to the gallery, then into the living room. I laid him down on a leather-covered settee.

"Get a sheet to cover him," I told Neil. And to Pete, I said, "Send for Doc Trego and Ace Wines."

Maria Sanchez lay, pale-faced and weak, on another sofa over near the front window. Her daughter sat beside her, weeping and shaken. I crossed to them.

There was a lump on Maria's forehead which Rosalia was dabbing carefully with a damp towel. I looked down and said gently, "Do you feel like talking, Maria?"

She nodded.

I said, "Tell me what happened — everything — since I left here this morning."

She struggled to sit up. I helped her and then sat down beside her. She touched the lump on her head gingerly. "Paul, he came first — not long after you go."

I nodded. "I saw him driving out as I went toward town."

"He and your father talk for a long time. I hear your father shouting, even though the door was closed. Then Paul went away. I went in to see if your father was all right. He was very angry."

"Then what, Maria?"

"He tell me to go out to the bunkhouse and get somebody to find Dave Franks. He want to see Dave right away."

144

"Then what?"

"I found Pete Hanley and he went after Dave. I do not know where Dave was, but he come here in about two hours. All that time your father sits in his office and looks at nothing. He is angrier than I have ever seen him. I am sure he will have another stroke. I ask if I should send for the doctor and he curse me!"

"Go on, Maria."

"Then Dave Franks he comes. He is with your father for about ten minutes. All that time your father is shouting. I am half scared to death, Dane! I am so sure he will have the stroke, so I stay out on the gallery, near his office door."

Rosalia brought her glass of water and she gulped it down. "Then I hear four or five shots, and a minute later Dave Franks comes running out the door. Almost he run into me. He hits me with the barrel of his gun, and that's all I remember until Pete and Rosalia they bring me to."

"All right, Maria. Thank you. Go on up to your room now and try to rest."

Pete crossed the room to the cupboard where the whisky was kept and came back with a bottle. He handed it to me and I took a long pull. I asked, "Why, Pete? Why?"

He shook his head helplessly.

Neil came downstairs with a folded sheet. He handed it to me and I shook it out and covered the old man with it. Then I went back to Father's office. Pete followed silently.

The answer had to be here. If it wasn't, then only Paul or Dave Franks could tell us what had happened.

I shoved the wheelchair aside and sat down on a corner of the desk. I picked up the papers there, and began to glance through them.

The answer was here all right, plain and brutally clear. There was an affidavit, signed by Ed Slaughter, testifying that he had seen Dave Franks and Tom Sunblade driving a herd of two hundred or more Sunblade cattle south through the hills near his ranch. There were other papers, bills of sale signed by Tom Sunblade, conveying in all nine hundred and thirty-two Sunblade cattle to the Alkali Land and Cattle Company of Los Santos, New Mexico. There was a bankbook on the Los Santos Bank, showing a balance in Tom Sunblade's account of $9,487.44.

It was all there. No wonder it had driven the old man wild with fury.

Paul Lasher must have spent considerable time and money accumulating this evidence. Why? Because he hated Tom? I didn't think so. There was another, deeper motive for what he had done.

Today, he had driven out here, obviously to lay his accumulated evidence before Father. And he must have known the terrible effect it would have on John Sunblade to discover that his favourite son was a thief — no, worse than a thief. Because Tom had stolen from his own father — from himself as well, in a sense.

I doubted if Paul could have foreseen that Franks, cornered and faced with incontrovertible evidence of his guilt, would kill the old man. But Paul certainly knew that Father had been warned by Doc Trego not to let himself become overly excited or angry.

I was appalled at the cold-bloodedness of it. Paul had deliberately tried to kill Father by gathering and presenting this evidence to him, instead of bringing it to me or taking it to Ace Wines.

I handed the papers to Pete and he glanced through them swiftly. I could see from his face that he was, step by step, reaching the same conclusion that I had reached.

He looked at me angrily. "The worst of it is that Paul will get away with it. There isn't a court in the territory that would do anything but turn him loose. You know and so do I that he killed John. But there's not a shred of proof."

I asked, "What does he want? Why did he want Father dead?"

Pete said, "He wants Sunblade — all to himself. When he gets that, he'll want something else. It'll never stop, Dane — not until he'd dead."

I knew that Pete was right. Paul Lasher was more dangerous than John Sunblade had ever been. John Sunblade had had a stopping point. There was nothing, apparently, at which Paul would draw the line.

CHAPTER
SIXTEEN

When Doc Trego and Ace Wines arrived, it was almost midnight. They came together, Doc driving his buggy, Ace riding a saddle horse behind it. Doc ran up the steps with his bag in his hand, but I stopped him at the door. "You can't help him, Doc. But you can write out a death certificate. And you can tell me how many times he was shot."

"Is that important?"

"It is to me. One shot is all it takes. I want to know what kind of man Franks really is."

Doc walked over to where my father lay, covered by the sheet. He peeled it back and drew up a chair. I turned away.

I looked at Ace and said harshly, "Have you caught him yet? Is your posse out?"

Ace lowered himself heavily into a chair, facing me. He sighed heavily. The lines of his flabby face were deeper tonight and there was something like controlled panic in his eyes. He said, "I've got a deputy heading up that bunch of your boys that Johnny Dolan brought in. It's snowing like hell in town, Dane. It's starting to snow out here. You can't expect miracles on a night like this. If we find him, it'll be luck. Nothing else. Funny thing, though. Paul said he saw Dave heading east, but I snooped around a little with a lantern before I'd let 'em go. I picked up Frank's tracks heading west."

Ace stopped and shook his head wearily. Then he said, "Why'd he do it, Dane? Why did Dave kill the old man?"

For a moment, I hesitated, instinctively wanting to protect Tom, I suppose. I handed the packet of papers to Ace and watched him read them. His eyes widened and his lips pursed into a soundless whistle. "Where's Tom? What if we catch up with him?"

I stared at him coldly. "Tom's out riding somewhere, I suppose. Probably spending the night in one of the line-camp cabins. Pete went after Dave so maybe he knows where Tom is. Just get this straight, Ace. You can have Dave Franks, if he's still alive when you get him. But I'll fight you all the way down the line for Tom. And if he's killed while you're trying to take him, you're going to answer to me."

Ace shrugged and got heavily to his feet. He watched me covertly, as though trying to gauge the temper and determination in me. At last he called, "Doc, if you're going back pretty soon I'll tie my horse on behind and ride with you. It's getting cold."

Doc was writing something, his bag propped up on his knees. He finished and looked up. "Shot five times, Dane. Every one of 'em was enough to kill him. Actually, the first one probably did it. The others must've been fired for spite, or out of fear."

I nodded. Probably there had been both spite and fear in Dave Franks as he triggered the gun. Old John

Sunblade was a legend. You couldn't blame Dave for believing it took more than one little piece of lead to kill a legend.

Doc said soberly, "You have my sympathy, Dane. Shall I tell Anne not to expect you for Christmas?"

I shook my head. "I'll be there. There's no use in pretending a lot of grief I don't feel. I never got along with him, especially after Mother left. But, God, Doc, the way he was killed! He was crippled . . . crawling on his hands and knees, trying to reach his gun. Franks must've watched him, and let him get almost to it. And then he cut him down."

Doc nodded, his face drawn.

I watched him and Ace leave from the gallery in front of the house. It was snowing harder now, almost assuring Franks of a clean get-away.

Pete was standing unobtrusively behind me in the doorway. I said, "Pete, you're foreman again. Now, where did you find Dave when Dad sent for him?"

"He'd been over at Pegleg. I knew he was there, so I rode that way after him. I met him about an hour or so away from here."

"How about Tom? Have you any idea where he is?"

Pete shook his head. "Probably at Pegleg too. He and Dave have been mighty damn thick the last few weeks."

"Then Paul will warn him off."

"Maybe. Maybe not. Neither of us knows what Paul will do,"

I was silent, thinking. Pete yawned. I told him to get some sleep.

150

I watched him leave. We'd have to have the funeral tomorrow afternoon because there weren't any undertakers in Ashlock. I knew Doc would make the arrangements, and the news would spread fast enough.

I turned out all the lamps but one, and trimmed that one until it gave off only a feeble glow. Then I climbed the stairs wearily and went to bed.

I couldn't sleep. Paul must have put a lot of work into collecting all that evidence, I thought. How had he been able to do it? How had he known Dave and Tom were rustling when I hadn't, even though I rode Sunblade every day?

The answer stared me in the face. Paul knew, because Paul had put them up to it. I remembered that it had been Paul who persuaded the old man to demote Pete Hanley and put Dave Franks into his place as foreman. This must have been why. As foreman, Franks could go where he pleased, answering to no one.

In a way, I'd played right into their hands, by slugging Tom that day in town, loading him onto a horse and delivering him to Dave Franks. Naturally he was pretty sore when he came to — sore enough to listen to any proposal Dave might have made.

I got up at dawn, without having slept a wink. I dressed swiftly and went downstairs and out into the frosty morning air.

During the night the snow had stopped and the clouds had blown away. This morning the land was dazzling white for as far as the eye could see. The sky was a deep and flawless blue.

I saddled a horse and mounted, warmed by his brutal jolting as he bucked the frost out of his body. Then I lined him out, loping, towards the south.

I was headed nowhere, and had no particular destination in mind. I wanted to think, and I always seemed to think better while I was riding alone.

The sun came up, and my eyes slitted against the glare. A band of antelope raced across in front of me, to disappear behind one of the numerous, rolling ridges. In every direction I could see the dark red shapes of scattered Sunblade cattle.

I thought of Tom, with pure amazement. Nine hundred head! More than thirty thousand dollars. And Tom had got less than ten thousand. Where had the rest gone? To Dave Franks? More probably, it had been split three ways, a third to Tom, a third to Franks and a third to Paul Lasher.

How far, or how long I rode that morning, I don't know. I paid no attention to the miles that rolled behind, or to the sun, rising steadily in the cloudless sky.

Still heading south, I crossed a trail of bunched cattle, traveling west. It was dimmed somewhat by drifted snow, but I could tell immediately that it was not the erratic trail of a bunch of cattle drifting through the storm. The wind last night had been out of the north, and cattle never drift crosswind.

Last night I'd been confused and bewildered. Now, anger began to rise in me, anger that grew with every stride of my horse. The sun rose higher as I followed

152

the trail, warming my back, starting the snow to thawing.

And the trail grew plainer until at last it was no longer fuzzed by drifting snow. I realized that it had not been made last night at all. The trail had been made this morning; right now it was not more than thirty minutes old. Tracks of several horses overlaid those of the driven cattle and in one place I came upon a pile of horse droppings still steaming slightly in the frosty air.

At about eleven o'clock, I cautiously topped a long, low rise and less than a mile ahead saw a bunch of perhaps seventy-five cattle being hazed along by five riders. I turned and, staying out of sight behind the slope, spurred my horse into a run. I circled the slowly traveling cattle, staying out of sight by riding down a long, natural drainage that roughly paralleled the course the cattle were taking.

I traveled thus for half an hour, galloping when I was safely hidden, traveling slowly when I was necessarily exposed. At last I reached a point of land from which I could look down at the approaching herd and near which they had to pass.

Tension mounted in me as I waited. Slowly, at a plodding, patient gait, the cattle moved toward me. I slid my rifle from the saddle boot and crawled up the ridge. Lying there, I waited, studying first one and then another of the approaching riders. Then I released an involuntary sigh of relief. Tom was not among them.

When they were two hundred yards away, I put the rifle to my shoulder and sighted carefully along its barrel. I fired. One of the rustlers slumped forward and then tumbled from his saddle. I fired a second time, and the horse of one of the others fell and lay kicking on the ground. Jumping up, his rider ran to the horse left riderless by the other and mounted.

Then the four spurred their horses and wheeled toward me, their six-guns drawn. I could have lain there and killed them all. I don't know why I didn't. Perhaps I wanted them to see me and to know who had hit them so unexpectedly. In any event, I got to my feet and ran back to where I'd left my horse. I vaulted to the saddle and, wheeling, rode down the slope toward the four charging rustlers.

They split, two to my right, two to my left, to get me in their crossfire, and close enough for revolver fire. I raised the rifle again, centred on the chest of a big, bearded man, and pulled the trigger. He tumbled backward over the rump of his horse.

Now, I was directly between the pair on my right and the single rider on my left. They opened up with their revolvers as I tried to race ahead and get out of their crossfire.

Someone shot wild and put a bullet into the mount of one of the two men on my right. The horse fell and rolled on him, and a high scream tore from his lips as he was crushed beneath the saddle. Then I was past and the two remaining riders came together behind me and turned to pursue.

But now three were down and only two were left. I rode almost to the cattle, which were now spreading out. Then I whirled and jumped from my horse to the ground.

I steadied on one of the approaching men, but my rifle clicked on an empty chamber. I threw it down and drew my revolver. I raised it and centered on one of the approaching men, waiting until he would be in range.

Something hit me savagely and suddenly on the side of the head. Then I was lying on the ground, my face half buried in mud and melting snow.

Only for an instant did my consciousness of cold and wetness last, and then the dazzling sun upon the thawing snow went out and the world turned black.

I awoke to utter quiet except for the steady drip-drip of snow water as it thawed from a sagebrush bush and dropped onto a at rock ten feet from where I lay. My head, as I raised it, seemed to split in two. I couldn't suppress a groan as I raised an experimental hand to touch the place over my ear where it hurt the worst. My hand came away slick and wet with blood.

My clothes were soaked, and now a chill made me shiver uncontrollably. I fumbled for my gun, found it not a yard from my hand, half buried in snow and mud. Looking around, I saw my horse unconcernedly pawing the snow a hundred yards away.

Painfully pulling myself upright, I examined the tracks about me, and knew that the pair had come and stood over me and decided I was dead.

The bodies of the three dead rustlers lay where they had fallen. I recognized none of them. The cattle had scattered out, grazing, until now they were no more than fifteen or twenty of them visible.

I found my rifle, wiped it off on the leg of my pants and then stumbled to my horse. I mounted with considerable difficulty. Head splitting, vision blurred, I reined the horse toward home.

Twice again before I reached the ranch, I crossed the plain trails of driven cattle.

The word of my father's death had traveled fast and the wolves were even now tearing at a dying Sunblade. Whoever was behind this was not wasting time.

CHAPTER
SEVENTEEN

As I rode into the yard at Sunblade, I saw that funeral arrangements had gone on without me. The yard was filled with buggies, buckboards, wagons and saddle horses, and both yard and house overflowed with Trujillo County folks come to pay their last respects to a man many had hated and few had liked, but whom all had respected for what he had carved out of Comancheland and held in spite of everything.

I saw Doc's black buggy and slipped in the back door through the courtyard to wash the blood and mud from my face in the kitchen. Maria Sanchez, her face frightened and sympathetic, her eyes red from weeping, brought me a clean towel and dabbed gently at the furrow over my ear.

"You mus' be more careful, *mi hijo*. The ranch, it need you now."

I said, "Thanks, Maria," and went upstairs, ignoring the people in the front room. Inside my room, I stripped down to the skin, towelled myself dry, and shaved in cold water. Then I put on clean underwear and a black broadcloth suit. I hesitated about strapping on the gun, but finally I belted it around me and went back down the stairs. Several people I knew slightly tried to stop me and offer condolences as I went through the living room toward the courtyard door, but I only nodded and did not stop.

The feeling of unreality, begun yesterday when I'd first seen Father's body, persisted even now. I felt strangely lost and alone. Father had ruled this house so long, dictating every move that was made, that his absence left a void I knew only time could fill.

Out in the courtyard, I stopped at the door to Father's office, and after a moment's hesitation, stepped inside.

Maria had scrubbed the blood from the floor where father had fallen, but the wheelchair still sat behind the desk. I looked around at the walls, at the varied assortment of trophies hanging there. A Comanche shield of tough buffalo hide — a lance — a bow and quiver of arrows — a warbonnet taken from a dead chief — the tanned hide of a gray wolf — a beaded buffalo robe. Over in the corner was a collection of old rifles, all of which Father had used to defend Sunblade at one time or another.

A wave of nostalgia engulfed me. I couldn't help remembering my boyhood awe as I'd stood here in the doorway and stared at these things.

Father had been different, then, more tolerant than in later years. As a small boy, I'd worshipped him even if I hadn't been able to get close to him.

I frowned, knowing my place was back in the big front room, accepting the sympathies of the countryfolk. But the sense of urgency, the feeling of time slipping rapidly away, was too strong.

158

I thought, *Let Neil do that. He's better at it than I am*, and left the office. I closed the door behind me, then went to the courtyard gate. From there I made my way to the bunkhouse, avoiding a few loiterers with a brief nod.

Pete Hanley stood just inside the bunkhouse door. Johnny Dolan had returned during the morning with his crew of man-hunters, and now almost the entire crew jammed the long bunkhouse.

I knew them all, by name at least, and waited for them to quiet down before I spoke. All were scrubbed, shaved and dressed in their best, and most were acutely uncomfortable.

I raised my voice so they all could hear. "Pete Hanley is foreman again."

Johnny Dolan, his young face concerned, interrupted. "What happened to your head, Dane?"

"Bullet burn. I surprised a bunch of rustlers."

Pete Hanley whistled soundlessly. "They ain't losin' any time, are they?"

"That's not all. On the way back here I crossed the trails of two more bunches being moved. It adds up to something pretty big."

They waited, eyeing me doubtfully. I knew that some of them had no confidence in my ability to fill my father's boots. I knew some of them were disloyal, that some had been doing what Deuce Laverne had done, accepting a cut on cattle stolen with their knowledge and consent. But until I could get other men on whom I could depend, I needed them — needed them all.

I said. "Right after the funeral, come back here to the bunkhouse, all of you. We'll see if we can't give these rustlers something they didn't bargain for."

For a few moments there was uneasy silence. Then a grumbling began at the rear of the room. A man said stridently, "Not me, by God. This outfit's licked. The old man ain't even buried, an' already they're tearin' it to pieces. I'll take my pay an' mosey along tonight."

The grumbling rose in pitch. Another man called, "Me too. Count me out."

I controlled myself with an effort. If the crew quit me, I didn't have a chance. I yelled, "I won't ask anyone to fight for punchers' wages! Anyone that stays draws double pay 'till this is over."

The room was bedlam now, with everyone talking at once.

I yelled over the noise, "Decide for yourselves what you're going to do! Anyone that wants to quit can draw his pay right after the funeral and leave."

It occurred to me suddenly that those who quit might help themselves to a bunch of cattle as they rode away, so I added, "One thing. Anyone that quits had better not be seen on Sunblade again. Is that clear?"

The only answer was a sullen silence.

I turned and went outside. Those who stayed would stay out of loyalty to Sunblade. Those who left would not have been swayed by pleading any more than they had by the offer of increased wages.

I saw Anne Trego come from the house with Doc, and walked toward her. Suddenly I felt alone and helpless. Father had lived out his life without liking or

160

trusting anyone. Now, when we needed our crew in order to exist, there was nothing to hold them except money, and that hadn't been enough.

Behind Anne and her father, I saw Ace Wines come from the house, immaculately attired, a politician's unctuousness about his expression. I knew I could expect little help from the sheriff in the days to come.

Sunblade Ranch had been John Sunblade, an old long-horned bull, king of everything he could see. When he'd been alive the wolves had kept their distance, afraid of his deadly horns. But now that the old bull was dead, they'd lose no time in trying to tear out his vitals. They were already tearing and slashing at the ranch. What could hold them off? What could turn them back?

I went toward Anne. My head throbbed painfully, and worry no doubt added to that pain. I kept the wounded side of my head away from her but she wasn't fooled. "Dane! You look terrible! What's happened to you?"

"I had a brush with some rustlers. Got creased, is all."

"You ought to be in bed!"

I shook my head. "I'll be all right."

Doc stepped from behind her and peered into my eyes. "You've got a concussion, Dane. It shows in your eyes. Head's splitting, isn't it?"

I said, "Whoever's after our hide was pretty careful as long as the old man was alive. But they've got the bit in their mouth now. And I can't go to bed. If I do, I'm finished."

Doc looked at me steadily for a moment. He glanced at the house. "Folks are going in the house again. I guess they're ready to start." He moved slowly in that direction without looking back.

I looked at Anne, and saw a new awareness in her eyes. Her voice as she spoke was suddenly small and timid. "How does a girl go about getting a man to repeat a proposal, Dane?"

I gripped her arms. "I'll repeat it, Anne. But not now. I don't know what's going to happen. If I married you I couldn't guarantee that you'd be safe. Give me a month. At the end of a month I'll know whether I've won or lost out here."

She laughed unsteadily. "Now you're putting *me* off." Her eyes held fear as they clung to mine.

I said, "Don't worry. Everything will be all right."

She shook her head. "I'm afraid it won't." She smiled with an obvious effort. "But you're doing the right thing, Dane. You're doing the only thing you can. You owe it to your father to try and hold things together." She paused, hesitated and finally said, "Just be careful, will you, Dane? Promise me you'll be careful."

Most of the people in the yard had now crowded into the house. The Presbyterian minister from Ashlock opened the service from the stairway with a prayer, and then Maria Sanchez played some church music on Mother's old organ. After that the minister said a kind of eulogy, which was mostly untrue. He made Father out to be a kindly, misunderstood man, sounding apologetic about his strength and ruthless determination.

It seemed to last forever, but it was over finally and the pallbearers carried Father's casket out to the waiting buckboard. The mourners formed a procession that wound out away from the house to the small family burial ground on the hill behind it.

The sun was setting as they lowered the casket into the grave with slings. The minister said a short prayer and the mourners filed away.

I stayed at the grave with Neil for a moment and looking across it, I saw Paul Lasher, Juanita and Chiquita standing there. Paul was studying me sharply, as though trying to read my thoughts. Juanita seemed anxious to get away. Chiquita watched me too, but with tears in her eyes.

I walked away, and Neil followed like a shadow. Paul left Juanita and caught my arm. "What are you going to do, Dane?"

I tried to keep the anger out of my eyes. "What do you think?"

He said soberly, "This has been a shock to you, hasn't it? Why don't you go away for a while? I could probably arrange a sale of Sunblade if you . . ."

I laughed sarcastically. "I suppose you could, at that. Don't bother. Nobody's selling anything. I like it here."

"Suit yourself, Dane," he said, a little stiffly.

I stood on the hill and watched the stream of vehicles crawl out of the gate. A number of the crewmen waited by the courtyard gate to be paid off, already changed into their riding clothes. I turned to Neil. "Part of the crew is quitting, Neil. Pay them off, will you?"

He nodded and walked down the slope to the house. I waited until everyone was gone. Then I went down the hill myself and entered the bunkhouse.

There were pitifully few men left there. Pete Hanley. Johnny Dolan. Four others. Discouragement stabbed me. Then I remembered how Father had looked, lying in his casket. I remembered how he had been in life. I knew these odds wouldn't have dismayed him; they would only have made him fight harder.

The sun was gone now and dusk crept across the land, darkening the interior of the bunkhouse. Pete wiped a match alight on the seat of his pants, lifted a lamp chimney and touched the flame to the wick.

In the guttering light it gave I studied the faces of the men before me. Pete was calm and unruffled, as though every day of his life he'd faced a similar fight for existence. Young Johnny Dolan, husky and brash, was grinning tensely with anticipation. The others looked vaguely uneasy as though they were appalled that so many had gone, and a bit uncertain of the wisdom of staying.

I said, "This won't be easy. You all know that. Double wages won't pay you for the things you'll have to do or the risks you'll have to take. But I'll tell you all this; I need you now. If any of you ever need me — for anything at all — I won't let you down."

I felt embarrassed by the depth of feeling within myself, by the depth of my gratitude to these few loyal ones. Pete probably sensed my embarrassment, for he said matter-of-factly, "What's first, Dane? What are we going to do?"

I said, "There's only one thing we can do, with the numbers we've got. Put three men out to patrol. The rest of us stay here. Whenever one of the patrols spots anything, they ride here. Then we go out and clean up."

"You going to turn them over to Ace?" asked Johnny.

I shook my head. "Ace is on the fence. We'll handle them ourselves. It's the only way we can do it."

CHAPTER
EIGHTEEN

At dawn on Christmas day, Sunblade began its fight for survival. Three men rode out, in three different directions. Pete, Johnny Dolan, Ross Neimeyer and I waited at the ranch.

Maria brought more coffee to the bunkhouse at sunup, and we sat around the table drinking it and playing penny-ante poker in virtual silence. Waiting was hard, for all of us felt that only prompt and ruthless action could halt the epidemic of rustling. I wasn't sure that so few of us could administer prompt and ruthless retaliation, but we were going to try.

Tension increased as the hours passed. At ten, I heard the distant drum of hoofbeats and ran to the door. From the west a rider came, thundering along as though the devil were at his heels.

Instantly all of us bolted for the corral. And by the time the rider, Sid Arnold, arrived, we had our mounts saddled, and a fresh one for him as well.

He shouted as he rode in, "Three men, Dane. Strangers to me. They've got twenty-five or thirty head, pushin' 'em west toward Pegleg."

He slid from his horse and I stripped the saddle off as Sid mounted the fresh horse we had saddled for him.

I turned the lathered animal into the corral and mounting, followed Sid from the yard.

We pounded along silently for nearly two hours, crowding our horses, for we knew they'd have to be strong when we reached the men we sought. Gone was all the indecision and doubt that had plagued me before. Gone was the irresolution I had previously felt.

It was, perhaps, significant that we overtook the three rustlers in the little draw I remembered from so many years before — the draw in which Tom had shot the nester and where he had been beaten so savagely. As Sid had said, they had between twenty-five and thirty cattle, mostly steers. They swung around in their saddles when they heard us coming, left the cattle they were driving and tried to get away.

One drew a rifle from his saddle boot and, hipping around threw shot after shot toward us, without effect. When they saw that we were almost certain to overtake them, they shunted back and forth a few moments and then split up. One rode up the slope toward the bluff above the draw, one headed straight up the draw, the other cut off toward Pegleg.

I yelled, "Pete, you and Sid take the one on the left. Johhny, you and Ross the one straight ahead. The one on the right is mine."

Immediately Pete cut away, with Sid thundering at his heels. Johnny and Ross tore straight ahead, visibly overhauling their quarry. I swung right and my horse bounded up the slope like a frightened deer.

Mine was the one who had emptied his rifle at us. Now it was back in its boot, and his revolver was in his hand. As he tore up through a break in the rim, he turned and fired at me twice. One of the bullets kicked up dust a dozen feet to my left. The other struck a rock and ricocheted off. Then he passed from sight behind the crumbling rim above my head.

I spurred savagely, and my horse bounded up through the same trail the rustler had followed. He had left behind a cloud of dust, slow to dissipate in the still air. For an instant it blinded me, choked me, and then I was through it and out on top.

I hauled my horse to a halt so swiftly that he reared. Almost in my very face the outlaw's gun barked, and I smelled the acrid powdersmoke and felt the muzzle blast. Then I released my hold on the reins, slipped my feet out of the stirrups and slid off the rump of my rearing horse.

I had my gun in my hand before the horse had dropped to all fours and galloped away.

The outlaw shot again, but he was panicked now, and shooting wild. His horse, visible from the corner of my eye, stood motionless a hundred yards away. I realized he had laid a neat trap, by dismounting the instant he reached the top, just as my finger squeezed the trigger and my revolver bucked in my hand.

The bullet smashed into the rustler's right shoulder shattering the bone, driving him back and half spinning him around. I recognized him suddenly as the stranger who had slugged me in LeClair's Mercantile earlier in the month.

168

I picked up his dropped gun and flung it over the edge of the bluff. I said harshly, "Get on your horse and get back down the hill."

Without holstering my gun, I started after my own horse. I caught him, mounted and rode back to the outlaw.

He stood beside his horse on the side away from me. And then, as I drew near, his rifle, which he had been hiding behind his horse's bulk, poked unexpectedly into view.

He rested it on the saddle, awkwardly holding it in his left hand and against his left shoulder. I could see his grayish face and pain-crazed eyes behind the gaping muzzle.

My hand streaked for my gun, and I spurred savagely. My horse leaped aside as the rifle roared, and then began to back.

I clubbed him down with the revolver barrel and then, raising the gun to eye-level, shot the rustler in the chest. He fell without a sound.

I dismounted and, leading my horse, walked to where he lay. That had been close — too close. In the future I'd treat them like trapped wolves. To hell with trying to keep them alive.

I ground-tied my horse and loaded the rustler's body onto his own horse with some difficulty. I tied him down with my lariat. When I got through my hands and the front of my shirt were covered with blood. I wiped my hands on the legs of my pants. Then, mounting, I led the horse with its inert burden back down off the rim to the tiny stream in the bottom.

Pete and Sid Arnold were already there, their quarry also dead and loaded similarly to mine. Two gunshots in the distance upstream told me that Johnny and Ross had just now caught up with the one they had pursued.

The cattle already were spreading out. Pete grinned a little shakily. "Been a long time since I had to kill a man." He was puffing nervously on a wheat-straw cigarette.

Sid Arnold seemed to be bothered not at all. He looked pleased, almost smug. "What now, Dane?"

Pete said soberly, "We'd better bury 'em as soon as we get back. Or leave 'em here for the buzzards. No tellin' what Ace might do when he sees them, or which side of the fence he'll be on by the time we get there."

I shook my head. "We're riding 'em into town, slung across their saddles. We're going to park 'em right in front of Ace's office. I want the whole town to see what we do to rustlers. It's the only chance we've got — scaring the ones that are still working at it."

Pete nodded reluctant agreement. He watched me for a long time, as though trying to read my thoughts and understand the things that lay behind my eyes. I knew he was weighing me against my father, trying to decide if I had John Sunblade's ruthlessness and implacability.

Looking around, I saw Johnny Dolan come riding in with Ross, trailing the third outlaw's horse. This one was still alive, but he died almost as they stopped before us, choking on his own blood.

We started back toward home silently. Killing was a grisly business, even when the victims were men like these.

170

I looked at Pete, riding soberly beside me. I said, "It's not just chance that these three happen to be here in Trujillo County right now. And they're not the only strangers hanging around. Somebody sent for them."

Thin, sterile winter sunlight bathed the bleak landscape. Overhead a light haze of cloud spread across the sky. Snow lay spotty on the ground. Ever present herds of antelope stared at us without fear as we passed. Jackrabbits bounded from our path. A hawk wheeled high above and a flock of ravens screamed raucously as they rose, startled, from some unidentified carcass.

Pete nodded. "Somebody sent for them, all right. And you know who it was."

"Paul?"

He nodded.

"But why? He's one of Pa's heirs. He'll get part of Sunblade. He doesn't have to steal from it."

"He won't be satisfied with part of Sunblade, the way I figure it. He wants it all."

"Stealing a few cattle won't give it to him."

I didn't see how Paul could get his hooks in Sunblade. I did, however, decide that I'd not make the mistake of underestimating Paul.

When we got back to the house, Maria and Rosalia had Christmas dinner ready, including turkey, roast-beef, ham, and all the traditional fixings plus a few of her own from below the border. Feeling a bit guilty about letting Anne and Doc down, I nevertheless ate until I could hardly move.

Afterward, Pete Hanley and I trailed the horses bearing the rustlers' bodies north into Ashlock.

We arrived in late afternoon. The sun was down, and the streets of the town almost deserted. But as we rode along the streets, I could hear doors opening, and startled voices.

We tied in front of Ace's office. He wasn't there, so I went across to the hotel and climbed to his room.

He'd been sleeping, fully dressed, on the bed. His face was flushed with Christmas cheer and his eyes were bloodshot. I said, "I've got something for you over at the office, Ace."

He followed me surlily down the stairs. Out in the street, he stopped and stared at the three horses with their inert burdens. He breathed, "God!"

I said, "Pass the word, Ace. That's what's going to happen to every rustler we catch on Sunblade."

He went on and unlocked the door of his office. He seemed confused and indecisive. I mounted and headed for the Trego's, calling back to Pete over my shoulder that I'd meet him at the hotel in an hour.

Dusk lay quietly over the town as I tied before Doc's house. Lamplight winked from the windows. Anne let me in, her face sombre, her eyes strange.

There was a Christmas tree in the parlor, a cedar cut from some shady draw and decorated with gilded gewgaws, strings of popcorn and candy, and tiny red candles.

Looking down at Anne I said, "I'm sorry about not coming for dinner. I hope you didn't wait for me."

She watched me steadily and at last she said, "You could have waited until tomorrow, Dane."

"For coming to see you?"

"You know what I'm talking about. I saw you and Pete trail those three dead men into town. This is Christmas, Dane."

"They were rustling on Christmas day! They can pay the penalty on Christmas day. I don't see what the hell . . ."

Anne said softly, "Dane, don't let's quarrel today. Come on. Let Dad give you a drink. And there's something under the tree for you, even if you are late."

Doc came from the kitchen, a glow in his cheeks, a couple of glasses in his hands. "Drink this. Good for winter chills," he said heartily.

I grinned, some of my defensive stiffness evaporating. I drank the whisky and took the package Anne handed me.

Inside was a pair of hand-knit woolen socks and a muffler to match. I laid them aside and took her in my arms. In her eager response was all of her own fear of the future, her desire to have at least this from me before something happened.

Doc groused good-naturedly, "All right, all right; I'll go," and headed back toward the kitchen.

Anne broke away, saying shakily, "Merry Christmas, Dane."

CHAPTER
NINETEEN

At full dark, I left the Trego's and made my way down the quiet street toward Saloon Row. When I noticed a light burning in Ace's office as I reached the intersection, I turned that way instead.

Ace sat at his desk. He scowled as I came in. And said sourly, "Folks been doing a lot of grumbling, Dane. You could have waited, damn it!"

Ace's repetition of Anne's criticism rubbed me raw. "Wait, hell! We caught them in the act! Christmas or New Year's or the Fourth of July, when I catch rustlers helping themselves to Sunblade cattle there's going to be trouble! You're the sheriff of this county, it's *your* job to catch these thieves yourself instead of criticising me for doing it for you."

"But . . ."

"But nothing! Who the hell got you elected? Sunblade did. And what have we ever asked in return? Have we ever tried to tell you how to do your job?"

"No. But damn it . . ."

"Maybe you need somebody to tell you," I went on. "Maybe you don't know without being told. You haven't even caught Dave Franks."

Ace flushed painfully. "You ride a man pretty damn hard, Dane!"

I calmed a little. "All right. I won't say any more. Anyway, I'm not asking you to clean up this rustling. We can kill our own snakes. But I want your backing and you'd better give it to me. If Sunblade folds this whole town had just as well fold too, you know that."

Ace grunted, "The town puts pressure on me too, Dane. They're saying that maybe those men weren't rustling at all. That I should lock you up and hold you for trial. They want me to charge you with murder!"

I laughed harshly. "Try it!"

I didn't want to look at this frightened, confused man any more. I slammed out the door and went into the street. I mounted and galloped toward the hotel. The drink Doc had given me only seemed to have stirred me up, and now I wanted more.

The Ashlock Bar was closed, but farther down, Dutch's Place was still going strong. I swung down, looped my reins over the hotel rail and went inside.

Pete sat on one of the lumpy leather sofas. He looked up instantly as I came in. There was an expression of acute concern in his eyes.

I said, "Come on, Pete. I'll buy you a drink."

Pete stood up. "Better stay out of Dutch's tonight, Dane. The town's all stirred up. I never seen such a collection of hardcases as there is in that saloon. Ace is scared to budge out of his office."

"Why?"

"That bunch is ugly. They're talking a raid on Sunblade. I went in there for a drink and I was glad to get out in one piece."

I felt reckless and stubborn. I was tired of being crowded, and criticized and opposed. I said, "I want a drink and I'm damned if a bunch of two-bit hardcases are going to scare me off. Coming?"

Pete shook his head. "*I'm* not that loco."

I went out angrily. I hadn't expected Pete to back away, and it infuriated me even though I knew the thing I was about to do was foolhardy. But I figured that if they ever got me on the run I was finished.

I went down the street and shouldered the door open. I felt foolish standing there glaring at the crowd, but I was committed now. I shouldered toward the bar.

Some of these men were former Sunblade punchers. Some were total strangers. A few belonged in the town. But in them all one quality was universal; they stared at me with smoldering dislike and distrust.

I reached the bar and called, "Whisky, Dutch." He looked at me carefully, then slid bottle and glass down the bar. I poured a drink and looked up to see him standing in front of me. "Dane, get out of here," he said worriedly. "This is no place for a Sunblade tonight."

I didn't answer. The man on my right had glanced suddenly at me as Dutch said "Sunblade."

Dutch wouldn't let it drop. "They're worked up over them three dead men you trailed into town today. Get out of here, or I won't answer for the consequences."

"Nobody asked you to." I downed my drink and poured another. As I lifted it, the man on my right

176

jostled me and the drink spilled down the front of my shirt.

I set the glass down carefully. Then I turned my head and looked at him.

He was a stocky man, short and enormously broad through the shoulders. His eyes gleamed with anticipation and there was a nasty smile on his mouth. He said, "Why'n hell don't you stay out of a man's way?"

I knew what was in his mind and how he'd build it up. If I tried to rough it up with him every man in the saloon would want to get at least one lick at me and they'd beat me to death.

I swung to look at the crowd. With my right side away from him, I snatched out my gun and, turning again, rammed the muzzle hard into his midsection just below the point where the ribs join.

He grunted, gasped, and bent toward me. His face turned a ghastly shade of gray. Hugging his middle, bent almost double, he slowly crouched, resting his back against the bar and hunkering on the rail. He sounded as though he couldn't get his breath. He'd suddenly lost all interest in me.

Not so the man on his right. With scarcely a glance at his downed friend, he grabbed for the gun at his thigh.

I didn't want to shoot, so I lunged toward him and brought my gun down in a chopping motion that caught his forearm. His gun clattered on the rail at his feet but did not discharge.

They were crowding in toward me now, a press of hostile bodies. In a moment more somebody would pull a gun and shoot. I lifted the muzzle of mine and fired at the ceiling. "Get back! Get back or the next time a bullet's coming right through you!"

They hesitated but could not push back. There were too many behind, crowding, pushing. There was a look in their eyes that turned my blood cold. It was an animal look, not of hunger but of unreasoning hatred.

Suddenly I realized I had been foolish and stupid to come here tonight. I had accomplished nothing. I was in a position where I was going to have to kill or be killed. Either way, I'd be finished. After tonight the pressure on Ace Wines would be such that he couldn't ignore it.

Abruptly, I turned and vaulted the bar at a bound. I struck Dutch full in the chest with both my feet. He slammed back against the backbar mirror and it shattered under the impact. Shards of glass showered down like icicles from a thawing roof in spring.

Dutch recovered and dove away, sprawling full length on the floor behind the bar. I ran the other way, crouched, expecting momentarily the smash of a bullet into my body.

A flurry of shots sounded, and bottles shattered beside me. Whisky poured down over me. Suddenly then, easily distinguished from the pistol shots, a rifle boomed — not a small rifle but a big one, a Sharps buffalo gun. Pete hadn't let me down.

I got to my hands and knees, ready to sprint for the back door. I heard Pete bellow, "Hold it, you sons! Or I'll put the next one right into the bunch of you!"

I eased to my feet as the room quieted. I saw Pete, head and shoulders poked through a smashed window, covering the crowd with the Sharps. I hurried to the back door, went through, shot the bolt behind me. Then I picked my way through the stacked cases and beer barrels until I came to the alley door. A moment later I was in the alley, and Pete was beside me, mounted, holding the reins of my horse in his hand.

I took them from him and swung to the saddle. Out in front I could already hear the shouts of the mob as they piled into the street from the saloon and began to run toward the alley.

Pete spurred his horse and we pounded out of town. I ranged up beside him and yelled, "I'm sorry, it was a fool stunt. Thanks for snaking me out of it."

His voice was oddly triumphant as he said, "There'll be some red faces in Trujillo County before this is over! There's more of the old man in you than most of them thought."

Chiquita Johnson was at the ranch when we arrived. She was waiting, pale-faced and subdued, in the huge living room, looking dwarfed and small on the enormous cowhide covered sofa.

Otherwise the room was empty. She got up as I came in and hurried toward me. "Dane, I've got to talk to you."

She was wearing a split riding skirt and a shapeless sheepskin coat. In her hand she held a battered Stetson hat.

"Sure, Chiquita. But aren't you an awful long ways from home?"

She nodded. "Dane — what happened out at the pond — don't think about it. You and Anne — well, you belong together I wouldn't want to think . . ."

I said gently, "You didn't ride all the way here to tell me that."

"No," she said. "I wanted to warn you. Paul is out to ruin you just like he did Pegleg."

"How do you mean?"

She shook her head. "I don't know exactly. But I do know he has a plan — besides all the rustling."

"You figure he's behind that?"

"I know he is. Every day strangers ride in to see him and ride out again. In the past week, he's talked to every one of Sunblade's neighbors, and to a lot of men from town. I don't like it, Dane."

"Anything else?"

"He's different with Mother. I thought he loved her when he married her, but he doesn't, Dane. He hardly ever sees her and when he does they fight."

I asked, "What do you know about those notes of Pegleg's? Anything at all?"

"I'm afraid I don't. But I'm sure he signed most of them while he was in Denver. And I think it was to cover gambling losses rather than money Paul actually loaned him."

I nodded. She looked tired and weak, so I drew her back to the sofa and made her sit down. "Have you eaten anything, Chiquita?"

"I'm not hungry."

180

"Coffee?"

"All right."

I found Maria Sanchez in the kitchen and asked her to bring in some coffee and a couple of cups. She did, along with some cold turkey sandwiches. Chiquita began to eat with hungry relish.

I said to her, "I appreciate your coming over here, Chiquita."

"Have I been any help?"

I nodded, though I'd guessed earlier pretty much everything she'd told me.

She said, "Then I'm glad I came. Have you heard anything from Tom? Have they caught Dave Franks?"

I shook my head, and she asked timidly, "Do you think Tom is really mixed up with Dave Franks? Did he really steal from Sunblade?"

I nodded. "No doubt of it. Why?"

She flushed, and turned her face away. "Nothing. I was just wondering."

I said harshly, "Stop worrying about Tom. He's really not worth it."

Her eyes flashed briefly, but she bit her lips and withheld her reply. I was sorry for her. I could see she was in love with Tom, and I doubted if Tom even knew she was alive.

I said, "Won't you stay over here tonight?"

She shook her head. "No. I'll go on home. Be careful, Dane." She hesitated. "And Dane . . .?"

"What?"

"Don't be too hard on Tom when you find him?"

I made my voice soft. "All right, Chiquita. At least I'll try not to be."

She smiled, and her eyes were bright. She went out, mounted, and galloped off into the night.

CHAPTER
TWENTY

It was nearly dark on the following day when I learned of the high-handed rustling in progress out on Sunblade's sprawling range. And when I did hear it, I could scarcely believe it.

Two of our patrolling punchers, Sid Arnold and Frank Marranzino, came in together, riding hard, so excited they could hardly talk. "It's something big this time, Dane," Frank panted, his eyes still incredulous and unbelieving. "Why, they're practically holdin' a roundup out there! Thirty men gatherin' and maybe ten or twelve holdin' the gather. They're movin' south toward Willow Springs. We figured they'd camp for the night at the Springs, so we come in."

Sid nodded confirmation. "I never heard of anythin' like it! They're workin' at it just like they owned the herd!"

I glanced at Pete Hanley and said wearily, "Our seven men aren't going to be much help, are they?"

Pete's eyes flashed. "You say the word, Dane, and we'll take them on. We wasn't looking for gravy when we stayed, were we, boys?" His glance at the others was challenging, but their agreement was half-hearted.

I said, "Pete, I wouldn't send seven men against forty. I'll send you south for help. I'll get money from Neil and we'll hire thirty or forty gunslingers of our own. Six of us ought to be able to slow this roundup down until you can get back with help."

I found Neil in Father's old office and said, "I want twenty-five hundred dollars right away. Write me a check."

Neil ran a hand through his thinning hair. "I can't sign a check, Dane. The old man always signed the checks."

"Well, give me cash, then."

Neil shook his head. "I can't. Sunblade is an estate now and Paul Lasher is the administrator. You'll have to see him. Besides, there isn't more than a couple of hundred dollars in the house."

I stared at him angrily. "How the hell did Paul get his hooks into us that way? Why aren't you the administrator?"

Neil said apologetically, "Father never had much faith in me. It was Paul he relied on. I suppose that's why he made Paul the administrator."

"Did he tell you he was doing that?"

"He didn't have to. There was a paper attached to his will naming Paul."

"What did the will say, for God's sake?"

Neil said, "It leaves Sunblade to the three of us, in equal shares. But it hasn't been probated and until it is, Paul's in charge."

I hardly heard him. "So now we've got to go to Paul for every damned dime we want! Is that it? What if he says no?"

184

"We don't get the money. But I rather think Paul will be reasonable."

"Don't count on it." I slammed out of the office, wondering how the devil Father could have been so blind.

I ran to the corral and roped out a horse. I saddled as fast as I could and rode in the direction of town. Time was running out fast. Willow Springs was about eight miles southeast of the house, and about eleven miles from our southern border. If they gathered as they went, they'd be off Sunblade and into the hills in another couple of days.

I didn't know how long it would take Pete to get some men and return, but it would be at least a week. Somehow we'd have to delay that roundup until the week was up.

I made it to town in a little more than an hour, but I nearly killed my horse doing it. I yanked the lathered animal to a halt in front of the Ashlock Bank Building, took the steps three at a time, and burst through the door. Paul looked up mildly from a desk piled high with papers.

Controlling my anger, I pulled up a chair and straddled it. "Paul, I need twenty-five hundred dollars. Our crew is down to six men and I've got to hire guns if I'm going to stop the rustling that's going on. They're out at Willow Springs right now holding a roundup just as if they owned the herd."

Paul smiled as though I were a small boy telling a tall tale. He said soothingly, "What do you really need the money for, Dane? If you'll tell me, maybe I can let you

185

have it. But hell, Dane, I'm administrator of your father's estate and responsible for it. I can't just pass out money recklessly to you even if you are one of the Sunblade heirs."

I asked as softly as I could, "Are you calling me a liar?"

"Look, Dane — a fantastic story like that . . ." Paul spread his hands in an eloquent gesture.

I said grimly, "You refuse, then?" I'd been a fool for coming here. The men out on Sunblade range were there because Paul Lasher had put them there.

He said, "I have to refuse, Dane. You can have whatever money you need for legitimate expenses, but after today I'm afraid I'll have to scrutinize everything pretty carefully."

I said harshly, "I could force you to give it to me. I could haul you into court and have you removed as administrator."

"That would take time, Dane," Paul said gently. "Months. But go ahead if you think you must."

He was right. Futile anger boiled in me. I turned and banged out of the office. There must be some way out. There had to be!

I changed horses at the stable and rode out of town, scowling with concentration. There was no doubt in my mind that Paul was behind all of Sunblade's troubles. If I didn't find a way to stop him there wasn't going to be a share of Sunblade for any of Father's heirs.

As I rode toward home, a plan began to grow in my mind. There *was* a way, all right. A desperate way — if

186

I wanted to take it. And I did. Because I knew it was the only way.

I was feeling better as I loped into the yard at Sunblade. I yelled, "Pete!"

He came running from the bunkhouse. "You get the money?"

"No, but there's another way. Get the men together."

I put my horse away and hurried to the bunkhouse. All of the crew was there — the few that were left. I rolled a smoke, lighted it, and swiftly outlined my plan to them.

When I was finished, they were all grinning. Pete said, "A couple of you come with me. We'll get the horses ready."

At dusk we ate a hasty meal, and at dark rode out of the yard, lining south toward Willow Springs.

While yet a mile away, I cautioned them all to silence. After that we rode quietly, the only sound an occasional squeak of saddle leather and the muffled sound of our horse's hoofs in the soft ground.

Willow Springs lay in a natural bowl that had been used for centuries by buffalo as a wallow. Now that the buffalo were gone, willows had grown up around it.

The cattle were bunched on the near side of the spring. In between, half a dozen campfires winked. Around them were a couple of dozen men. I supposed the others were night-herding.

With us, in addition to our mounts, was another horse which Pete had readied. There was a shapeless burden on his back, that occasionally clanked softly when he moved.

Luckily, the night was black as pitch, the stars hidden behind a thin overcast. Great clouds of frosty breath rolled from the nostrils of our horses. I said softly, "All right, spread out in a line."

They spread, to right and left, and we rode quietly down the grade toward the resting herd. Pete held a rope secured to the saddle pack on the extra horse, and I held the animal's halter rope. When I could plainly see the edge of the herd a quarter mile ahead, I said softly to Pete, "All right, let it go."

He yanked the rope, and I quickly slashed the halter rope with my knife. I had barely time to close the knife and slip it back into my pocket.

Then, with a deafening clatter, the burden Pete had lashed to the horse crashed to the ground. The horse jumped. As it passed me I laid the end of the halter rope savagely across its rump. The horse squealed and plunged toward the herd.

Behind the terror-stricken animal banged a wired-together string of tin cans, cowbells and kitchen pots. At each jump that crashing abomination seemed louder.

Keeping pace with the wildly running horse, the rest of us surged ahead, yelling, firing our guns.

And then, rising slowly above this racket, came the sound for which I had been waiting. At first it was low, like distant, barely audible thunder somewhere on the far horizon. But it swelled and grew until it filled the air. The sound of stampeding cattle.

I was riding now at top speed, spurring my horse with every jump. Ahead were the cattle and around me

188

rose a cloud of dust, the smell of fear, and the sound that seemed almost tangible.

Somewhere off to my right a horse screamed as he was overrun. And I realized suddenly that I was passing Willow Springs, for I saw the looming bunch of willows on my right. Then I smelled the smoky tang that could only have come from the ground-out embers of campfires. *Right through their camp!* I thought exultantly.

I yelled, "Pete!" but my shout was lost in the thunder of a thousand stampeding cattle.

I pulled at my horse's reins, but the animal had caught the contagion of the stampede and fought for his head. I heard another horse's terrified neigh and immediately following it the groaning of a man. I brought my horse to his haunches, sliding, my hand rough and heavy on the reins. Circling, I found the down horse and not far from it a shapeless lump that had been human. Dismounting, I knelt and struck a match.

Relief ran through me. It was one of theirs.

I rode on, then, more slowly, and gradually the noise of the running herd faded from my ears as it disappeared into the dark distance ahead. But I kept going, and at last, near the hills which marked our southern line, I saw a tiny fire wink in the pitch dark.

I approached with caution, but it was Pete who hunkered beside the fire, Pete and a couple of the others. I rode in, followed shortly by the other three who made up our crew.

Pete was grinning triumphantly. "All here, Dane, and not a scratch on any of us. What do we do now?"

"Nothing until dawn. Then we'll gather four or five hundred of what the rustlers had bunched and head them south. There's that Army Fort about ninety miles away and if we can get there before Paul realizes what we're doing, I can sell them to the Commandant. He knows me and he'll buy without asking a question."

Frank Marranzino began to chuckle. "Them cans an' cowbells sure as hell worked. I never heard such a godawful racket."

A line of gray now marked the eastern horizon. I said, "Anyone see what happened to the horse?"

Frank chuckled again. "He's all right. Probably headed back toward home by now. The cans and stuff busted loose as he went through the willows at the Springs."

The sky in the east turned lighter gray, and half-light began to drift like smoke out across the empty land. I knew the rustlers would be too demoralized to do anything much before midmorning. They'd be gathering up their dead and helping their wounded.

Squatting there, soaking up the welcome warmth of the tiny fire, I knew something else. The lines were drawn and from now on my fight with Paul Lasher would be out in the open. When he heard what had happened last night he'd be like a rattler that's prodded with a stick. He'd strike back viciously.

We stayed at the fire until the sun's rays came sliding down the hills and beat against our backs. Then we stamped out the fire, mounted and began to gather strays.

These were docile cattle, spent from their night-long run. And as the sun mounted higher in the cloudless sky, the bunch before us slowly began to grow.

At nightfall, I had tallied four hundred head. I said, "That's enough. Tomorrow we'll trail 'em south."

CHAPTER
TWENTY-ONE

On New Year's Day, I rode back onto Sunblade land. With me were five men of the crew, and in a money belt strapped around my waist was over twelve thousand dollars in currency. I had left Pete Hanley at the Army Post with more than a thousand dollars of the receipts from the cattle. He was to recruit a gun-fighter crew and return as soon as possible.

Riding into the yard, Johnny Dolan asked, "What're you goin' to do with all that money, Dane?"

"I don't dare bank it or Paul will get hold of it. I guess I'll just have to carry it around for a while."

"Hadn't you better cache it somewhere?"

"Later. Right now I'm beat."

If I had taken Johnny's advice, it would have saved me a lot of trouble. Instead, I headed through the darkness toward the house. Although it was late, light still gleamed from the windows.

Neil's still up, I thought, and opened the ponderous front door.

Neil sat before the fireplace, staring vacantly into the crackling fire. As I came in he glanced up. I saw the fear and warning in his face too late. I spun around, hearing the door slam behind me. I shot my hand toward my gun, but before I could close it on the gun grips, my wrist was seized in a savage hold.

The hard muzzle of a gun rammed savagely against my spine and Ace Wines' voice growled, "Don't do it, Dane. I wouldn't want to have to shoot."

I flung myself aside, tearing my wrist free from Ace's grasp. I struck the floor rolling as Ace's gun blasted. The bullet tore splinters from the floor beside my head.

I yanked my own gun from its holster and tried to bring it to bear, but just then I banged into a table and lost a precious second while I struggled against the unexpected obstacle.

I came to my knees, and saw that Ace was not alone. He had three others with him, carrying rifles. Ace yelled frantically as they raised them, "No! Hold your fire!" and dived directly into the muzzle of my gun.

I had the hammer back and my finger on the trigger, but I didn't shoot. I couldn't. Instead I tried to swing the gun as a club.

Ace charged into me and bowled me back. My swinging gun struck him on the shoulder, and then his own gun came down against my skull.

The back of my head struck the floor and for an instant flaming balls of red revolved before my eyes. Then all was dark and still.

There was a dry fuzzy taste in my mouth and an abominable ache in my head. My body felt bruised and sore. I didn't know it then, but the soreness was from bouncing to town on the bare plank bed of a wagon and then sleeping off the head blow on the cold stone floor of the Ashlock jail.

I stirred, rolled, and tried to get up. I could hear voices dimly and tried to focus my dazed mind on the words. I groaned, and the sound seemed to come from somewhere across the room . . .

Raised on elbows and knees, I shook my head, concentrating on the words I heard. ". . . hell you can't, Ace. You let me in there to see him. He's been out pretty near twelve hours. You want him to die? He could, you know. And if he does, I'll stir up so damn much trouble they'll hear it clear to the Capitol."

"All right," came grudgingly from Ace. "Go on in. But no funny stuff. He's in on a rustling complaint, filed by Paul Lasher. Things are changing around this country, Doc. Sunblade ain't a magic name no more."

I heard Doc say drily, "Don't tear your pants jumping back and forth across the fence you been straddling, Ace." Then I heard a key in the lock and Doc came into the cell.

I grinned at him foolishly, still dazed by pain, and said, "Give him hell, Doc."

Doc helped me up to a bench. He examined my head and peered closely into my eyes, one after the other. He said sourly, "You're just as hard-headed as old John was. That ought to've cracked your skull but it didn't."

He turned and yelled irascibly at the Sheriff, "I'm not going to slip him a gun, Ace! Stop standing there gawking and get me a pan of hot water."

Ace growled, "Ain't no hot water in the jail. I'll go across the street to get it but I'll have to lock you in with him while I'm gone, Doc."

"All right! All right! Just get at it."

194

The door slammed shut and the lock squeaked. After a moment I heard the outer door slam. Doc said hastily, "You've got yourself in one hell of a mess, boy. They've confiscated all that money you had on you. They've got a rustling charge against you that's bound to stick. Lasher's trying to get evidence enough to back up a murder charge, too."

I said, "Doc, a man can't steal what already belongs to him."

Doc shrugged sympathetically. "The law says those cattle didn't belong to you yet. They belonged to your dad's estate."

Anger stirred in me. "I couldn't fight the rustlers without money, and Paul wouldn't give me a dime. I did the only thing I could."

The outer door opened. Ace came in with a dishpan half full of tepid water. Doc took it, saying sharply, "This boy needs rest and sleep, and he can't get it on the floor. Go get him a cot."

Ace went back out, grumbling, "By God, anybody else that gets throwed in jail can sleep on the floor. But not a Sunblade. It ain't good enough for them!" But when he returned he half dragged, half carried, a rusty iron bunk, and an armful of ragged blankets.

I felt better, lying on the cot. Doc finished bandaging my head and closed his bag. "I'll bring you some clean blankets."

"Thanks, Doc."

Doc left, and I closed my eyes wearily, filled with despair. My mind darted back and forth endlessly, seeking a way out of my predicament. Paul had the money I'd gone to so much trouble to get, and I knew he'd go on with his wholesale looting of the ranch. Tom was gone and if he was caught now there wasn't much I could do to protect him. Neil sat out at the ranch like a tame rabbit, taking Paul's orders. He'd warned me last night, but he hadn't had the guts to take a hand and help me.

Then I thought of Pete. He'd be back in a day or two, with a bunch of gunslingers. He had money enough for their first month's pay.

I closed my eyes, despair evaporating from my mind, and went to sleep.

It was dark when I awoke. Light from a lamp in Ace Wines' front office filtered through the bars and laid a pattern against the stone floor. I could hear muted voices in the street outside, then the door opened and I heard Anne say, "I've brought Dane some supper, sheriff."

Ace growled, "I doubt he's awake. He wasn't when the deputy took his regular supper in."

I sat up hastily and ran my hands over my bewhiskered face. I knew I looked like hell and it angered me that Anne would see me this way, dirty and unshaven and beat.

The light moved and came toward the cell door. Then I saw her, trim and neat in a long heavy coat and carrying a steaming platter that looked half as big as she. The smells that emanated from that platter were tantalizing ones for a man who had eaten nothing in over twenty-four hours.

196

Doc came behind her with blankets, and behind Doc was Ace, carrying a lamp. He set it down inside the cell and left. Anne gasped when she saw my face. "Dane! You look awful!"

I said, "I expect I do."

Anne gave me the tray, then sat down beside Doc on the bench. There were tears in her eyes.

I ate ravenously. When I was finished I looked at Doc. "Is Pete back yet?"

Doc said, "I haven't seen him."

I lowered my voice. "He's bringing help when he comes. I left him over a thousand dollars of that cattle money."

Doc said uneasily, "That's good."

Anne came over and sat on the bunk beside me. "Don't worry, Dane. Don't worry. You're alive and that's all that matters."

As dirty as I was, I didn't intend to kiss her, but she pulled my head down and kissed me on the mouth. Then she got up. There were tears in her eyes again as she said, "Come on, Dad."

I got up and walked to the door with her. My head began to pound again. From both Doc's and Anne's manner, I guessed something was wrong. I wanted to force them to tell me what it was, but I was too beat out to make the effort. It would have to wait until tomorrow.

They left, and I fell down on the bunk and went instantly to sleep.

When I woke again, the sun was streaming into the window, and Paul Lasher stood beside the bunk, looking down at me. His eyes held triumph and mockery.

I got up, angered as much by his immaculate appearance as I was by the expression in his eyes. "Come to gloat?"

His voice was conciliatory. "There's no use hating me, Dane. I only do what I have to do. I've got a responsibility to fulfill as administrator of your father's estate. Besides that, your father owed me a substantial sum of money and I've got to protect it. Surely you . . ."

I said furiously, "You damned thief, he didn't owe anybody a dime, least of all you."

Paul smiled patiently. "Do you think I'd make a claim like that if I didn't have the notes to back it up?"

I said, "How much?"

"Almost a hundred thousand."

Shocked, I said, "Get out of here, Paul, before I tear you apart."

Ace spoke nervously from the other side of the bars. "Don't try anything, Dane."

Paul edged to the door. "Open up, Ace."

Ace opened the door and Paul stepped out. I went to the bars and looked through at him. It gave me little satisfaction to know that I'd scared him. I said, "I don't know how you worked it, but I suppose you got your hooks into us the same way you got them into Pegleg. You're the one that put Dave Franks up to getting Tom involved, aren't you? And then when you had enough evidence against them you took it to the old man. Did you know Dave would kill him, Paul? Or did you figure the old man would get worked up enough over Tom stealing from him to have another stroke?"

Ace muttered to Paul, "You don't have to listen to this, Mr. Lasher."

"Wait. Let him finish, Ace."

I said, "I know now why you brought in all those damned hardcases. You didn't want us to have enough cattle left to redeem your notes and you didn't want us solvent enough to borrow it from a bank. Well, it won't work, Paul. You're licked whether you know it or not. Pete Hanley stayed in Arizona to hire a bunch of guns. When he gets back . . ."

Paul smiled blandly. "He's already back, Dane."

I must have looked startled.

Paul's eyes were gloating. "I sent that crew of gunslingers packing, Dane. It wasn't hard. All I had to do was tell them they could keep what Pete had paid them but that there wasn't going to be any more."

I looked at Ace. His face confirmed what Paul had said. I turned around and walked away.

It was over, and Paul had won. By the time I got out of this jail cell, Paul would have Sunblade sewed up tight. He'd call for payment on his notes, and when it wasn't made, the ranch would go up for public auction. Paul would bid it in for the face value of his phony notes and that would be that. Tom and Neil and I wouldn't get a dollar out of it.

Paul had forgotten just one thing. He wouldn't live to enjoy the ranch he'd stolen. No matter how long I had to wait, sooner or later I'd get out of jail. And when

I did, I was going to kill Paul Lasher. Even if I hanged for it.

They were still standing at the bars when I turned around. I thought Ace looked at Paul a little doubtfully, and I thought there was an appraising quality in his eyes as he glanced at me. I knew what was going on in his head. He was trying to make up his mind once and for all which of us was going to win.

I said, "Ace, you're going to have to get off the fence. Throw in with Paul or throw in with me. But I'm warning you — if you throw in with Paul I'll run you out of the country with your tail between your legs."

Paul laughed. "Talks big for an unwashed jailbird, doesn't he?"

Ace frowned and turned on his heel, and I went back and sat down on the bunk. I heard Paul leave, heard the door slam behind him. I heard his voice droning at Ace in the office.

I lifted the bench quietly and placed it under the window, which opened in the alley. I stood on it and peered out through the bars.

Down at one end of the alley I saw a match flare, saw the shadowy figure of a man as he lighted a cigarette. Glancing the other way, I thought I saw another man there, though I could not be sure.

I got down off the bench silently and replaced it where it belonged. I scowled angrily. Paul was taking no chances. Those were not Ace's men in the alley; they were Paul's, there to kill me if I managed to break out.

I sat down and tried to think. Paul held a good hand. I was beat if I stayed here, dead if I tried to escape.

I thought of my father and wondered what he would have done in a like situation. One thing was sure, he wouldn't have given up. He would never have admitted defeat.

CHAPTER
TWENTY-TWO

For a while there was silence inside the jail. Then I heard the outside door slam, and again heard the drone of voices. I supposed the night man had come to take over for Ace.

I thought that when Ace left, I'd try and get that deputy in here. But I shook my head. Ace was no fool. Neither was Paul. I could be sure of one thing; if I got away, it would be because they wanted me to.

The hours passed, and near midnight, Ace and the deputy came back into the jail. Ace asked, "Anything you want, Dane?"

I shook my head, and they returned to the front office, leaving the door to the cell-block open. I heard Ace's "Good night," and then the street door slammed. I heard the slap of cards as the deputy shuffled them and began to play solitaire.

And then, close on the edge of town, a coyote yipped. I sat bolt upright, and a grin started at the corners of my mouth.

I got up and went to stand under the window. Pete Hanley's coyote talk was good, but to me it was just the voice of an old friend. Pete had taught me that coyote talk before I was ten.

Standing on my toes, I peered out the window. I saw a horse briefly silhouetted at its far end. I could no longer see the man I'd spotted there before.

I left the window and went to the door. The deputy's hands were visible to me as he played the cards on the desk before him. I waited.

After what seemed an interminable time, I heard a knock on the street door. The deputy grumbled something, and his swivel chair creaked as he rose. He walked to the door and put a hand on the knob.

The door must have been pushed violently inward, for I saw the deputy come staggering back, off balance, falling, but still trying for his gun. Then Pete Hanley came into my range of vision, a gun in his hand. "Don't do it, man! Don't make me shoot!"

The deputy was now out of sight, but he must have decided against the foolishness of drawing against Pete, for there were no gunshots. Pete said crisply, "Johnny, get his keys and let Dane out."

I heard the jangle of keys and Johnny Dolan came into the passageway, grinning cheerfully, "Think we was never comin', Dane?"

I said, "Johnny, there's a man at either end of the alley."

His grin didn't waver. "Ours. Come on, Dane. Let's go."

Pete came along the corridor, herding the deputy before him. He tied the man's hands behind him with a piece of rope. He pushed the man onto the bunk and tied his feet. Then he stuffed his mouth full of pieces of cloth torn from the blankets and bound the gag in place with another strip, tied behind his head.

"Let's go," he said.

I followed silently. The jail had no alley entrance, but it did have a passageway beside it leading to the alley. Pete led and I followed and Johnny Dolan followed me. A man who had been lounging outside the door in the street brought up the rear, and this was gaunt, unsmiling Ross Neimeyer.

Frank Marranzino waited at the end of the passageway with four horses. We mounted and rode down the alley at a silent walk. Far behind us I heard another horse, and knew it was either Sid Arnold or Al Schwartz, and when we reached the mouth of the alley, another silent, dimly seen horseman joined us.

A warm feeling ran through me, one that made my throat feel tight. Every one of the punchers who had stayed after Father's funeral was here. It was a thing Paul had not counted on, one place where he'd guessed wrong. He hadn't thought that these six men, all that remained of Sunblade's crew, would risk their own safety and freedom for a lost cause. He'd failed to understand how strong loyalty can be in some men.

We headed north, led by Pete, and rode in utter silence until the town lay miles behind. Then I called, "Where we going, Pete?"

"The mountains."

"You got a particular place in mind?"

"I was thinking of an abandoned mine about five miles this side of Quartzite. One of the boys can ride into Quartzite for supplies, come morning."

This was as far as they had planned. They had no scheme for fighting Paul Lasher or for redeeming Sunblade. All they had wanted was to get me out of jail, even if they made outlaws of themselves doing it. I swallowed and cursed softly under my breath. Finally, I said, "I can think of a better place, Pete. Tom and I used to go to an old cabin up this way, an old cow-camp cabin that hadn't been used in years. It'd be better for us because there's grass and water for the horses."

Pete grunted assent. I took the lead, groping back over fifteen years as I tried to remember the trails Tom and I had taken to reach the place.

We passed through groves of mighty spruce, whispering gloomily in the light, cold breeze. We passed through quakie pockets from which the leaves had gone and now lay underfoot like a golden carpet, covered in spots by snow, exposed in others.

We climbed steadily, and as we did, part of my mind was on the trails, remembering them and the landmarks on either side, but the other part was on Sunblade.

There was only one way out, as far as I could see. Paul Lasher was the key to the whole business. Alive, he would win. He'd take Sunblade away from us and there was nothing I could do to stop him. But dead . . . I clenched my teeth against the cold, and shivered lightly.

Dawn was a gray feather, tracing the jagged line of peaks to the east when we rode into the meadow and looked across at the dilapidated cabin. The grass here was thick and long, and completely covered this morning with a heavy, hoary layer of frost.

The north slopes were heavily covered by snow, but the flats and the south slopes were almost bare. A stream tumbled noisily through the meadow, and where beavers had made their dams there was an opaque layer of ice on the surface.

The cabin was made of logs, half buried in the far slope. And a horse on picket grazed fifty feet away from it, barely visible in the cold dawn light.

I reined up, dismayed at the unexpected development. I said softly, "Somebody already here."

Pete said, "One man is all."

I hesitated briefly. Then I said, "Circle your horses round in back of the cabin. Leave them and come in on foot. When you're set, Pete, yip like a coyote. I'll ride in openly and call out. If there's trouble, close in on him from both sides."

They rode away, and for a long time afterward I sat my horse in silence, half hidden in the fringe of timber surrounding the meadow. The scent of pine needles filled my nostrils as the sky grew lighter in the east.

I was appalled, suddenly, as I looked down the trail the Sunblade crew and I were beginning to travel. Already we were wanted men, outlaws. And now we were stalking this cabin, prepared for violence. I wondered where it would stop, and if it ever would . . .

A sudden noise at the cabin drew my eyes, and I saw a thin plume of smoke begin to drift from the chimney. Then Pete's coyote talk began behind the cabin and I put my horse in motion, heading out across the meadow towards the cabin. I splashed through the stream. My horse was laboring up the far bank when a shot split the silence.

I abandoned the horse instantly and flung myself, belly down, on the bank. Without raising my head, I yelled, "Hey, in there! This ain't no posse! Put up the rifle and come on out."

For an instant there was no sound from the cabin. Then, faintly, came the thumping, banging sounds of a fight taking place inside.

I tensed to rush the place and had just gained my feet when the door flung open and a familiar voice bawled, "Dane! Come on. It's all right now!"

That was Tom's voice, and that was Tom in the door. Behind him I could see someone prone on the floor.

Tom was grinning from ear to ear as I approached. He looked sheepish too. From both sides of the cabin the crew came, silently, watchfully.

Tom stepped outside. "Damn your eyes, Dane, I'd be glad to see you even if I thought you were goin' to hang me. What's the old man goin' to do, make me serve a stretch in jail?"

I stared at him blankly. "You mean you didn't know?"

"Know what?"

"That the old man's dead? Dave Franks killed him."

"Dead? Franks?" Sheer amazement and unbelief crossed Tom's face. It took a minute for his mind to absorb what I'd said. Then he turned savagely, pawing for his holster, his face ugly with rage.

I pinned his arms behind, while Pete and Johnny crowded into the cabin. They yanked the prone man to his feet. It was Dave Franks, his mouth bleeding where Tom had hit him.

I said, "Easy, kid. I need Franks. And besides, I want to see him hang."

Tom's jaw was hard. He seemed bigger now, harder and more heavily muscled. The sullen defiance that had been a part of him so long was gone.

I said, "Paul Lasher has got his hooks into Sunblade. But if Franks will talk . . ."

Tom yanked free. "He'll talk," he muttered. "He'll tell us every damn thing he ever knew. I'll see to that!"

All of us went into the cabin, and closed the door against the frigid air. Pete pushed Franks into a chair in the corner. Al and Ross began to look through the cupboard beside the stove, preparatory to getting breakfast.

Tom walked over to Franks. He hooked a leg of Franks' chair with his boot toe and yanked. The chair crashed to the floor, spilling Franks against the wall. Tom walked to him and kicked him savagely in the belly. Franks shouted with pain and humiliation.

Tom kicked him again, and Franks groaned. I felt a growing sickness in the pit of my stomach. I almost said, "Quit it, Tom," but I caught myself. Franks was groaning steadily, hugging his belly and rolling around on the floor. Tom snarled, "Get up," and booted Franks hard on his butt. Franks got to hands and knees. Tom yanked him up the rest of the way, holding him with one hand, swinging with the other. The blow landed on Franks' nose and it spurted blood. Franks made no effort to fight back.

208

Tom swung again and again and at last, in disgust, released Franks, who collapsed to the floor. Tom kicked him in the groin, and Franks screamed like a woman.

I gritted my teeth as Tom waited. When Franks quit groaning, Tom said, his voice icy with restrained fury, "You make me sick at my stomach. But being sick ain't going to make me quit. The only thing that'll do that is for you to talk. So get at it. Right away."

Franks looked at him, and tried to get up. Tom kicked him again. "Talk from where you're at."

"It was Lasher," Franks said. "He talked me into it. He told me if I got you in it with me the old man couldn't touch me. But Lasher double-crossed me. He got affidavits and bills-of-sale from the people that bought the cattle and turned them over to John."

"So you killed him."

Franks didn't reply. I looked at Tom and said, "All right, Tom. Let up. Let's eat and get started."

Pete asked, "What you got in mind?"

"Ace Wines is the key to the whole thing. We take Franks to him and see that Franks repeats his story, so that Ace will stay out of it. Then we go out to Sunblade and wait. Paul will have to get rid of Franks and me. So he'll come after us. And when he does, we'll be ready for him."

"With eight men?"

I nodded. "With eight men."

Not one of them flinched. Ross dished up the grub and we all ate. Then we saddled the horse we'd seen picketed in the meadow, and another we found behind the cabin in the trees, and started back toward town.

We traveled slowly, resting our horses often, so that we would arrive after dark. At five-thirty, we arrived at the edge of town.

I knew the chance we were taking was a slim one. Even if we got to Ace, I had no assurance he'd listen. Perhaps Paul had already bought him. But I knew we had to try.

At this time of evening, in early January, it was nearly full dark in Ashlock. The sky held only enough light by which to see the silhouettes of the false-fronted store buildings along Main.

Lamps winked from the windows of saloons, stores and homes. The mud underfoot was growing hard from frost.

I left the others at the edge of town with instructions to come running at the first sign of trouble and, with Tom, Franks and Pete Hanley, rode along the valley toward the jail.

Tom said, "I know Ace like a book. You can set your watch by him. At five on the nose he goes to Dutch's for his drink. At five-twenty he goes back to his office and stays 'til six. He'll be there now. I'd bet on it."

We dismounted behind the jail and left the horses tied to a fence. Then we slipped silently along the passageway toward Main.

There was no one visible in the street. I flung open the door and jumped inside, my gun in my hand. Tom pushed Franks in after me and he and Pete crowded in behind.

Ace half rose from his chair, his face sagging with surprise. "What the hell is this?"

I said, "Dave here wants to talk."

Tom turned and hit Franks in the mouth. "Go ahead, Dave."

Franks looked at Ace beseechingly. Tom hit him again. And then Franks talked. He told Ace everything he'd told us.

I said, "Now get on one side of the fence or the other, Ace. Right now. I'm going to hold Sunblade and I'm going to kill Paul Lasher. I want you to stay out of it."

Ace was a beaten man. He said, "All right, Dane. I'll lock Franks up."

I shook my head. "No you won't. We're taking him with us. He's the bait in our trap. All I want you to do is tell Paul we've got him out at the ranch. The rest is up to Paul."

CHAPTER
TWENTY-THREE

I sent the men out with Dave Franks, telling them I'd be along later, and then I concealed myself a half a block down the street from the jail. I didn't wait long. Ace blew out his lamp and came outside, locking the door behind him.

He looked up and down the street and then ducked his head and hurried down the street toward the bank.

He went into the building entrance. I waited a bit longer, and then I saw the light in Paul's office go out. A few moments later both of them came out. Ace crossed toward the hotel. Paul went into the Ashlock Bar.

Immediately I mounted and rode to the bank, glad there was no one in the street. I didn't want to be recognized by anyone just now.

I tied my horse in the shadows beside the bank and took the stairs at a run. Paul's office door was locked. I stood back and kicked it, hard, beside the knob. It banged open, the lock broken.

I crossed to the window and pulled the shade carefully so that no light would show through. Then I thumbed a match alight and touched it to the lamp wick. The lamp chimney was still warm.

I looked around, remembering this room from the day Pegleg Johnson had been killed here. I picked up the lamp and crossed to Paul's desk.

I had no idea what I was looking for. Something — anything that might prove Paul to be what I knew he was — in court.

I thumbed through his papers for the better part of an hour, finding nothing. Every now and again I glanced nervously at the door, but I heard no sound.

Down in the street now, I occasionally heard a shout. The evening's revelry in the saloons was beginning. Or so I thought.

Disgustedly, I got up from the desk. And then I remembered something. I remembered that Father had once found a paper he'd lost behind one of his desk drawers.

I yanked out the drawers, one by one. And at last I found what I needed — a simple thing, but one that told the whole story — how Paul had stolen Pegleg — how he'd planned to steal Sunblade.

It was a single sheet of white scratchpad paper, and upon it was the name *Russell J. Johnson* written again and again, on both sides. I'd seen Pegleg's signature several times in my life, full of curlicues and flourishes, and this signature was nearly identical with it.

No man sits and signs his name over and over on a scratchpad. Only a man trying to forge another's signature does that.

For a moment I was stunned. By forgery, Paul had stolen Pegleg, had brought about the fight that caused Father's stroke and led to Pegleg's death. He had also, undoubtedly, forged the paper designating himself

Father's administrator, and the notes he claimed to hold against Sunblade.

I didn't know much about such things, but I was sure that forgeries could be proved forgeries, once they were suspected.

Anger built in my mind. I wanted to go down into the street, find Paul Lasher and kill him. But I knew it wouldn't do. There was too much anti-Sunblade feeling in Ashlock and in all of Trujillo County. I had only recently escaped from jail. The thing for me to do was to ride out home. Paul would attack. I knew he would because he had to. He must know now that he'd have to kill both Dave Franks and me or lose everything he had schemed for and built.

I blew out the lamp and ran down the stairs. The street was no longer deserted. Several men were leaving Dutch's Place and heading downstreet toward the stable. Down there lanterns were burning and half a dozen men stood in their light, waiting beside their horses. Paul had lost no time. At dawn he and his bunch would be out at Sunblade, ready to attack.

I left town by an obscure route to avoid running into any of Paul's men, and rode at a brisk trot toward home. The wind was strengthening, and it had a cold, damp feel to it. Snow began to fall before I had gone a mile. By the time I reached home at eleven, the snow was over four inches deep and still coming down hard on a driving wind.

Anne Trego must have left town shortly after I did, for she arrived at Sunblade driving Doc's buggy a little

214

before twelve. Her face was wet and chilled, her clothing soaked by melting snow.

We were ready for Paul, not knowing if he would wait until dawn or not. As Anne approached, a man stepped silently up beside her buggy on either side and caught the horse's bridle.

She cried out, startled, and I recognized the sound of her voice. I went out and helped her down, and said impatiently, "Anne! What are you doing here? We're expecting trouble."

She laughed, almost hysterically, with relief. "Then you know. I wasn't sure you did. When I saw all those men getting ready in town I had to come."

"I'm glad you did. Now come on in and thaw out."

Inside the door, she came to my arms and lifted her wet face to be kissed. She was shivering almost uncontrollably. I led her over to the fire and slipped off her soggy coat.

I said sternly, "Doc must have been out of his mind to let you drive out here alone on a night like this!"

"He didn't know I was coming."

Neil came down the stairs. He was dressed to go out and carried a suitcase. He said, "I'll drive Miss Trego back to town. I'm leaving anyway."

I knew this had been inevitable from the first, so I didn't try to talk him out of it. "Let us know where you are, Neil. And write if you need anything."

He nodded, then crossed the room and gripped my hand. His voice was hoarse, and his hand trembled. "Good luck, Dane."

I said, "Don't worry about anything."

He tried to smile and failed. He turned to Anne. "Ready?"

She shook her head. "I'm not going. But will you tell Dad I'm here and that I'm all right?"

He nodded. He glanced at me once, hesitatingly, then went out the door into the storm. Maybe he'd find elsewhere what he'd failed to find on Sunblade. I hoped he would.

Anne stepped close to me. "What kind of chance have you got, Dane?"

"A fair chance, if he doesn't bring more than twenty or twenty-five men. And I don't think he will."

She put her arms around my neck. "And it will be all over tomorrow?"

I nodded.

She smiled, but there was uncertainty and fear in her eyes. She said shakily, "Then I'll wait until then. But I'm warning you, Dane Sunblade, I won't wait any longer than tomorrow. Now go on out and do what you have to do. And do it well."

I kissed her hard and went outside into the driving snow. I could pick the men out in the yard plainly. The snow made plain targets of men that would have been nearly invisible without it.

I ran back into the house. I took the stairs two at a time, and a moment later returned with a pile of sheets. I passed them out, and waited while each man cut eye-holes and donned his camouflage. I left each one cursing sourly, but as I returned through the yard a few moments later, I could pick out no single one of them even though I knew exactly where they were.

Beside the woodpile, I stopped to talk to Tom. "Cold, Tom?"

"Some. I wish to God they'd come."

He was silent for a long time. At last he said, "You know, Dane, now the old man's dead and it's too late, I'm sorry for a lot of things I've done."

I didn't reply, and a moment later he went on, "He was hard, and tough on the three of us, but . . . well, there was times . . ."

"Sure there were."

"Would you let me come back, Dane? Would you let me help put the place back in shape?"

I told him yes.

"You going to marry Anne?" he said then.

"Tomorrow, if things turn out all right."

He squeezed my shoulder. "Some of these days maybe I'll find a girl . . ."

"Sure you will." I was thinking of Chiquita, and remembering her concern for Tom.

I heard the confused beat of horses' distant hoofs just then and whirled to look toward town. I saw them coming, not a quarter mile away, a dark, moving blur of movement that rapidly increased in size as they thundered toward us.

Tom called anxiously, "Get out of sight! You stand out like a sore thumb in those dark clothes!"

I didn't move. I wanted to draw them right into the yard, right into the midst of the men I had stationed here. If they got cagey and surrounded the place, we wouldn't have a chance.

They whirled through the gate. I drew my gun and fired into their midst. Then I turned and ran toward the house.

Out there, a horse went down, kicking in the snow. The bunch hauled up and stopped, but when no more bullets came out of the dark, they moved again, thundering across the yard toward me.

Paul yelled, "It's Dane! Get him!"

A gun flared out there, and another. A bullet ricocheted off the woodpile and went singing away into the snow. Another cut a furrow at my feet.

Then they were close behind me, gaining so fast I saw they were going to ride me down.

I dived, rolled, and threw an arm across my face as the horses pounded over me. A hoof caught me in the thigh, numbing it instantly. I scrambled to my feet and began to run again, limping now. The horsemen were past me now, and were shooting at the house. They pulled to a halt fifty yards from it and for an instant milled there uncertainly. Ducking behind a building I yelled, "Let 'em have it!"

A hail of lead poured into the ranks of the attackers. The first volley emptied half a dozen saddles, the second another three or four. In this interval, I made it to the house and ran along the covered gallery. I burst inside, snatched up my Winchester from beside the door and punched out a window with its barrel. They were scattering now, but I brought one down.

They broke, then, less than three minutes after they had thundered through the gate. They spurred back out, and as they went, guns flared from the shrouded

218

men out there in the snow; and two more tumbled out of their saddles.

I slammed out the door. Figures materialized out of the snow as Sunblade's crewmen shed their sheets. They ran toward the barn, drawn by Pete's hoarse "Get after 'em! Ride 'em down!"

I crossed the yard at a run, realizing suddenly that I didn't know what Pete had done with Dave Franks. I bawled at Pete, "Hey! What'd you do with Franks?"

"He's tied up in the office!"

I stopped, and returned across the yard, cautiously avoiding the downed men. Some of them might only be wounded and still dangerous. I looked for Paul, but I didn't see him.

I went inside and closed the door behind me. Anne stood there in the cold gray of early morning's light, her fear gone, her eyes warm and soft now that I was safely back. I said, "The waiting's over. It's downhill from here on."

"Paul? What happened to Paul?"

"He must've got away." Worry touched me briefly. If Paul had got away, it wasn't over. Not yet.

Suddenly another thought occurred to me. I whirled away from Anne and crossed the room at a run, with Anne close at my heels. I burst through the outer door and into the courtyard. It was empty, but I didn't slow down. I tore along the gallery and flung open the door to Father's office.

Dave Franks sat in a chair behind the desk, his hands tied behind him, his feet tied to the legs of the chair. I breathed an involuntary sigh of relief. Then Anne burst in behind me, crying: *"Paul's coming!"*

I grabbed for my revolver, but the holster was empty. I'd lost it out front, rolling in the snow. And I'd left the rifle behind when I ran out here. I plunged across the room toward Pa's old gun, hanging on the wall.

I didn't make it. Paul came through the door, a gun in his hand. He shot, and the bullet showered my face with dust from the plastered wall.

I stopped. I turned and faced Paul. He was looking at my empty holster.

I said, "Ride on, Paul, while you can. Leave the country and I won't try to stop you. But don't be a fool. Dave talked to Ace and told him the whole story. I know those notes were forgeries and it can be proved."

Paul said, "Get away from him, Anne."

Her voice was a cry. "No!"

I said, "Do what he says, Anne."

She stepped away from me, moving over against the back wall of the office, out of my range of vision. She said, "Paul, put that gun down."

He didn't answer her. He just kept on looking at me and the hate in his eyes surprised me. This was personal with him, as much as anything else. He was going to enjoy killing me.

I tensed, waiting for the muzzle blast, for the heavy bullet's shock. I heard a small movement from Anne behind me, a small noise, and I recognized the noise because I'd heard it so many times before. It was the slight sound Father's gun made being lifted from its holster on the wall.

Anne gasped, "Dane! Catch!" and I whirled, dropping as I did.

Paul's gun made a roaring sound that filled my ears, and before it had died away I felt the smooth walnut grips of Father's gun in my hand. Dropping, falling, I couldn't stop or catch myself.

Paul fired again, and this time the slug hit me in the thigh.

I was slammed against the floor and my gun driven out of line. I steadied myself, stopped all movement, and centered it again on Paul. I squeezed the trigger and heard the gun roar.

Black powdersmoke billowed from its muzzle, filling the room with an acrid cloud. I felt dizziness and weakness from the thigh wound overwhelming me, and tried to raise the gun again.

But there was no need. Paul Lasher was standing, slumped, his gun hanging limply by his side. His fingers slacked and the gun clattered to the floor. Almost as though he were tired, he backed to a chair and sat down weakly. His head flopped to one side and his mouth hung open as he breathed his last. Dave Franks watched silently, his face white with terror.

Anne threw herself to the floor beside me. "Where are you hit, Dane?"

"In the thigh," I said. "Don't look so scared. Father took . . . a dozen worse than this, and look how long he lived. How many kids he raised."

Anne stared at me for a long time, as though her eyes could not get enough of me. Then she said softly, "He raised a man, too."

She touched my lips with her own soft ones and then got up and ran for bandages and water. Waiting for her to return, I began to grin to myself. Maybe the fight for Sunblade wasn't over. I doubted if it would ever be over, really. But now there were two Sunblades here to carry on, Tom and myself. In a year or two, there'd be even more.

Over against the wall, my father's wheelchair sat. I stared at it. I was weak from loss of blood, but suddenly I had the feeling that he was sitting there staring at me. There was approval in his harsh old eyes, and the faintest of smiles on his thin stern mouth.

Then Anne came back and I turned my eyes to her as she knelt and began to wash and bandage my wound. I couldn't help grinning. This was my wedding day, and I felt real good.

THE END

ISIS publish a wide range of books in large print, from fiction to biography. Any suggestions for books you would like to see in large print or audio are always welcome. Please send to the Editorial Department at:

ISIS Publishing Limited
7 Centremead
Osney Mead
Oxford OX2 0ES

A full list of titles is available free of charge from:

Ulverscroft Large Print Books Limited

(UK)
The Green
Bradgate Road, Anstey
Leicester LE7 7FU
Tel: (0116) 236 4325

(Australia)
P.O. Box 314
St Leonards
NSW 1590
Tel: (02) 9436 2622

(USA)
P.O. Box 1230
West Seneca
N.Y. 14224-1230
Tel: (716) 674 4270

(Canada)
P.O. Box 80038
Burlington
Ontario L7L 6B1
Tel: (905) 637 8734

(New Zealand)
P.O. Box 456
Feilding
Tel: (06) 323 6828

Details of **ISIS** complete and unabridged audio books are also available from these offices. Alternatively, contact your local library for details of their collection of **ISIS** large print and unabridged audio books.